THE FIRST MAGNIFICENT SUMMER

R.L. Toalson

VICTORIA

ALADDIN

New York London Toronto Sydney New Delhi

ALADDIN
An imprint of Simon & Schuster Children's Publishing Division
1230 Avenue of the Americas, New York, New York 10020
First Aladdin hardcover edition May 2023
Text copyright © 2023 by R.L. Toalson
Jacket illustration copyright © 2023 by Svetla Radivoeva
For information about special discounts for bulk purchases, please contact Simon & Schuster
Special Sales at 1-866-506-1949 or business@simonandschuster.com.
The Simon & Schuster Speakers Bureau can bring authors to your live event. For more information
or to book an event contact the Simon & Schuster Speakers Bureau at 1-866-248-3049 or visit our
website at www.simonspeakers.com.
Designed by Heather Palisi
The text of this book was set in Freight Text Pro.
Manufactured in the United States of America 0423 FFG
2 4 6 8 10 9 7 5 3 1
Library of Congress Cataloging-in-Publication Data
Names: Toalson, R.L. (Rachel L.), author.
Title: The first magnificent summer / R.L. Toalson.
Description: First Aladdin hardcover edition. | New York : Aladdin, 2023. | Audience: Ages 8 to 12. |
Summary: Twelve-year-old budding writer, Victoria spends a summer with her estranged father and
his new family which does not turn out the way she imagined.
Identifiers: LCCN 2022022760 (print) | LCCN 2022022761 (ebook) |
ISBN 9781665925495 (hardcover) | ISBN 9781665925518 (ebook)
Subjects: LCSH: Fathers and daughters—Juvenile fiction. | Family life—Juvenile fiction. | Self-
confidence—Juvenile fiction. | Diaries—Juvenile fiction. | CYAC: Fathers and daughters—Fiction. |
Family life—Fiction. | Diaries—Fiction. | LCGFT: Diary fiction.
Classification: LCC PZ7.1.T587 Fi 2023 (print) | LCC PZ7.1.T587 (ebook) |
DDC 813.6 [Fic]—dc23/eng/20220531
LC record available at https://lccn.loc.gov/2022022760
LC ebook record available at https://lccn.loc.gov/2022022761

To all the ones who were left behind

by the people they loved most in the world

Be your magnificent self

THE FIRST MAGNIFICENT SUMMER

WHITE
(Innocence)

Arrange whatever pieces come your way.

—Virginia Woolf

Period (noun): a length or segment of time.

The word <u>period</u> can indicate short stretches of time and also longer stretches, such as the Renaissance <u>period</u> (those dresses seemed a little over the top, if you ask me; if a person wore one of those during a Texas summer, she'd die of heatstroke); geological time, like eras and epochs; or the dividing of a school day into <u>periods</u>—but it's summer, and as much as I love learning (don't tell Jesse Cox), I don't want to think about school.

A period can seem incredibly fast, like the time Jenny took me to Rockport with her family and we swam and fished and ate seafood for every meal like no one cared about the cost of anything. A period can also be completely interminable, like the hours and minutes ticking up to the moment when you'll see your dad for the first time in two years.

*T*hat clock on Memaw's wall must have magnets made for my eyes, because I couldn't stop looking at the swirling black hands and Roman numeral notches. Six o'clock. Six thirty. Seven o'clock.

Two hours since Mom dropped us off. Two and a half. Three.

More than enough time. She was supposed to call when she got home, so . . . why hadn't she called?

My chest burned like the grass fire Jack accidentally started in Memaw's backyard last summer, and rubbing it didn't make it feel any less fiery. (We managed to get the grass fire out before Mom and Memaw got home, thank goodness. But the soles of our shoes were never the same after that.) My leg vibrated under the table, unusual for me.

I am a Stillness Queen. I can be still as stagnant water, as a hammock on a windless day, as the suffocating air every time Coach Finley makes us run to the T (my least favorite thing to do when school's in session).

Must be my nerves. Or maybe the quiet at the table. Or all the thoughts piling up around me.

I'm not supposed to open my journal at supper, but tonight I did, just to have a place for all the nervous energy to go.

"You don't want your spaghetti?" Memaw nodded toward my bowl, which I hadn't really touched. Another thing that's unlike me: not eating Memaw's spaghetti. It's the perfect blend of salt and tang, better even than Mom's homemade sauce. Mom says Memaw salts everything to death. I guess I like everything salted to death, then.

I didn't answer Memaw, but she kept right on talking, like maybe she was as nervous as I was. Am I nervous? I haven't reached a definitive conclusion yet, but I think yes, maybe I am, yeah, probably.

"Nerves, is it?" Memaw glanced at Jack. His brown eyes studied the table. His mud-colored hair curled around his ears like it does every summer. Mom doesn't waste money on haircuts when we're on break. I know why that's important, but I have to admit, it makes Jack look a little like a shaggy dog.

Maggie pushed her orange bowl forward, and the bottom of it scraped the wood in a way that made me wince. (A nails on chalkboard kind of sound.) "I finished mine," she said.

"Want some more?" Memaw said. Her eyes gleamed. I think Memaw gets a lot of joy out of feeding people. Or maybe it's just making people happy in any way she can. Mom says she spoils us, coming to visit with bags full of kettle-cooked chips and cream horns and new crossword puzzles for Jack and composition books for me and color ing books for Maggie. I just think she's the best grandma ever. (And I have four of them.)

Maggie nodded. "Yes please?" Her words arched up like she was asking a question.

"Maybe Tori will let you have hers." Memaw eyed me with that one raised eyebrow, her dark eyes blinking questions.

I shook my head and stuffed a forkful of the salty spaghetti in my mouth. "Not sharing," I said around the noodles. The salt was divine. A burst of intense flavor hit my tongue, and it made me wonder why I'd waited so long to eat.

Jack stuffed a bite in his mouth too.

Memaw said, "You bring all your notebooks with you, Tori?"

Do I ever go anywhere without my notebooks? I didn't

ask this question out loud because (1) it's not exactly polite, and (2) Memaw already knows the answer. She's the biggest supporter of my budding writing career, and without her I might not have volumes and volumes of my own stories and diaries. (I prefer to call them journals; people—Jack and Maggie—like to steal juicy diaries, but no one's interested in boring journals.)

I also didn't tell Memaw that I've decided to go by Victoria this summer. I've been Tori for twelve years of my life, and I'm ready for a change. A more grown-up name. Something to prove I'm not a little girl anymore. I'm still in a training bra, while all my friends have become women and moved up to the regular bra section, but at least I will have a new name. I mean, it's an old name given twelve years ago, but it's new for me. And grown-up. And womanly.

It's not a conversation for the supper table, so I let it go.

"All two of them," I said instead.

Memaw blinked at me like she'd forgotten her question. I do this all the time—I get tangled in my head and let a question sit way too long without an answer, and then the person forgets what they even asked. I was about to remind her she'd asked if I'd brought all my journals when she said, "Only two?" Her black eyebrows shot up even farther. "That enough for a whole thirty days?" She seemed to be saying something more underneath the words. Something like *Thirty days with your father? Thirty days away from home? Thirty days of no routines and unpredictability and anxiety-inducing newness?*

I try exceptionally hard to hide my weirdness from the world. (Mom says I'm quirky, not weird, but she's my mom. She's supposed to think I'm ordinary. Brilliant, but ordinary.) But Memaw is like one of those thermometers you wish you didn't have in Texas, the ones that you can't help but notice as you're walking out the gym door for another run to the stop sign a whole sweaty one-point six miles away from the school, the ones that practically shout, "It's one hundred one degrees out here, get back inside, you moron!"

She always sees right through me to the temperature inside. Sometimes it's kind of a relief. It's exhausting putting on a show all the time. Pretending you're perfectly fine when you're not.

Sometimes, though, it's a great big pain.

"I brought some books to read too." My voice sounded a little squeaky, like even I didn't believe I'd brought enough simple pleasures to distract me from less-than-ideal circumstances.

Okay, so I like routine and predictability and things that are old, not things that are new. And maybe I have a teensy little problem with anxiety that's hardly worth mentioning.

I shrugged, because, well, words are hard, and so is the truth.

Memaw stood up and disappeared into her room. Jack shot me a Look, but I couldn't decode it. I can't read many of Jack's Looks anymore, not like I used to. Middle school changed things for us in a weird and sometimes annoying way, but I don't like to think about that. So I don't. I let him have his football friends and band buddies and lunchroom chewing chums and leave him well enough alone, like he told me to do on my first day of sixth grade, when he was a big seventh grader on campus and I mistakenly thought that didn't mean anything special.

Memaw reappeared and plopped down a pile of composition books. "That enough?" she said. I spread them out. Two purple ones (Memaw's favorite color), one turquoise one (my favorite color), and three yellow ones (no one's favorite color but bright and hopeful all the same). Six notebooks for thirty days, not counting the two I brought.

"Yeah. Sure," I said. "Thanks."

I wondered, briefly, how she'd found the composition books so fast. Her room is a minefield of messy stacks and future Christmas presents and powder spilled on bathroom counters. I don't go in there often. Clutter ignites my anxiety like little sisters ignite annoyance.

I'm sorry. That was mean. Maggie doesn't deserve that . . . usually.

"Give you something to do while you're visiting your dad," Memaw said, folding herself back in her chair.

Memaw even looks like the perfect grandma. She's short and lumpy, with curly black-and-white hair that frames her face and neck in a halo. Her gray-brown tortoiseshell glasses are the kind that darken in the sunlight so you can't see her eyes. (I know the names of all the frame colors and styles of glasses, which is how I know Memaw's are tortoiseshell, because I spent two years trying to convince Mom to at least get me new glasses if she wasn't going to get me contacts. My old frames are held together with superglue, and one earpiece falls off every time I so much as adjust their position on my nose. Glasses are expensive, though, which is probably why I finally wore her down just in time for this summer, and now I am the proud owner of brand-new soft contacts. Clear ones. Mom said no to colored contacts, even though I tried to tell her that's all anyone wears anymore. She raised an eyebrow and said, "You really think I'm gonna let you get lenses that make you look like a cat?" Like I would do that. I just wanted blue ones. But Mom shook her head to even that. "Blue's not all it's cracked up to be," she said. She doesn't know, though. Her eyes are the same brown as mine, so how would she?)

Enough with the random brain detour, let's go back to the table and Memaw's "Give you something to do while you're visiting your dad."

The way she said, "your dad," its squeezed-up, clenched-tight sound, made it obvious to any but the most oblivious observer (Maggie is one of those. No, that's mean. Maggie's just . . . blissfully unaware. She has an excuse—she's nine) that Memaw does *not* like Dad. If my memory can be believed (and of course it can), she never has. She's never come out and said it, but you can see that kind of thing on the face, hear it in the voice, watch it in the stiffness of a back, if you're the right kind of nosy. Which I am.

I nodded again but didn't say anything. The grandfather clock in the living room chimed its half-hour song. Seven thirty. In exactly twelve hours, he would be here.

My throat tightened as hard as Memaw's eyes.

Good thing there's *Tales from the Crypt*, Memaw's favorite show, to distract me. If what's happening tomorrow doesn't make it impossible to sleep, creepy skeleton heads jumping out of coffins will.

(Memaw would be in so much trouble if Mom knew she let us watch *Tales from the Crypt*. It's not exactly a kid's show—bloody and gory and too spooky for imaginations like mine. And it's probably in the top ten reasons I still sleep with a night-light. Mom barely approved *Sabrina, the Teenage Witch*, and I had to practically beg her to let me watch *Friends*. But Memaw's house is a house of freedom and horror.)

July 15, 7:42 p.m.

*J*n twelve hours, he'll drive up in a shiny waxed truck that doesn't clatter, with a ceiling that doesn't sag, with four doors that swing right open without sticking, wearing that smile.

Truthfully, I don't know what he drives or if it clatters or sags or sticks or whether he'll smile when he pulls into Memaw's driveway. I haven't seen Dad in more than two years, and the last sighting was only for a hasty goodbye, in front of a house that was never ours, its "for rent" sign already stuck in the sloping yard. Dad just acted like it was any old regular day. Maybe to him it was. To me it was The Worst Day of My Life . . . but you live to be twelve, and you learn there are days much worse than The Worst Day of Your Life. For example, last year, I slipped on a wet spot in the cafeteria and slid all the way into a table where the most popular boy in school, Bran Martin, was sitting with his friends. They all looked at me and then said, at the exact same time, "Safe!" A baseball reference, ha ha. I thought for sure that was the worst life could get. And then I tripped all the way down the stairs after my induction into the National Junior Honor Society, with two hundred eyes on me. Worst Day. There are many Worst Days in life. You learn to wave at them as they pass by.

In twelve hours, Dad will drive us from Texas to Ohio, where we spent a year trying to patch together the cracks in our family. (Turns out some cracks can't be patched but actually get bigger and bleed all over the place until you have to admit that you're not a crack-fixer.) We'll be his for thirty whole days. The last time I saw Ohio, it was out the back window of The Boat (the ugliest green car in existence, I swear). It retreated from me in hills and valleys and green fields that led to Amish farmland, and I have to admit, the only words that filled my mind (besides all the ones related to Dad, which I don't want to record here, for keep-the-hope editing purposes) were "Good riddance." I thought I'd like the snow, after the suffocating heat of Texas, but it turns out snow gets everywhere, and it's just frozen water that melts and freezes you from the inside out. So yeah. Good riddance. Now we're headed back to Ohio. At least it's not winter.

Truthfully, Ohio wasn't all that bad, even the snow. (Mom would disagree; she hated scraping ice from the car before leaving for work.) Sure, I unintentionally rolled down a snowy hill in my brand-new birthday dress that year and, when I finally skidded to the bottom, sat there crying for a while (I was ten, and I cared way too much about pantyhose, but in my defense, it was snowing and cold and pantyhose are warm until they have holes), but all in all, it was an okay year. Except that what Mom promised ("If we move to Ohio, where he's working, he'll be home all the time") didn't happen. Dad didn't come home.

In twelve hours, I will fill in the gaps of What Dad Looks Like. It's not that I've forgotten completely. I still see a vague impression of him when I close my eyes: long legs, brown skin, eyes the color of grass on its way to dying in the pastures that mark this part of Texas. His face isn't exactly clear, though, and neither is his voice. Calling isn't Dad's strength, apparently. He has other strengths. Baking the best buttermilk biscuits, drinking a mason jar of milk in one breath, and sporting a Speedo (the kind professional swimmers wear, which is mortifying when you're his daughter at the pool party and all your friends are staring and you're hiding your face, hoping he dove in fast enough that they didn't notice he's swimming in what looks like underwear).

Truthfully, I wonder if forgetting is the brain's way

of protecting the heart from something painful. But that sounds like something Virginia Woolf might say. (I brought the fourth volume of her diaries with me this summer, snuck it right off Mom's bookshelf. I don't think she'll notice, but it did make my suitcase noticeably heavier.) Virginia Woolf also said, "Nothing has really happened until it has been recorded," which is why I keep a detailed journal. I've brought two blank composition books with me for the trip, plus the six Memaw gave me, and I'll record dialogue and events as accurately as I can. But I'm only human, so of course the following pages, which I'm calling "The First Magnificent Summer with Dad" (because hopefully there will be more) with the subtitle "A Record of Victoria Reeves, twelve years old" (in case anyone finds them after I'm gone), will be full of opinions and one-sided stories and hopefully absolutely no surprises because I don't like surprises, not even the good ones.

In twelve hours, my knees will maybe stop shaking, my heart will maybe stop this ridiculous thrashing, and my eyes won't burn so much, staring down the clock, and Dad will say all the things I know he meant to say that day we waved goodbye. *I'm sorry for what I did, I still want to be a family, I love you.*

Truthfully, I should probably know by now that things don't really ever work out the way you think they should.

July 15, 7:46 p.m.

*Y*ou kids know what you'll do in Ohio?"

I closed my notebook for a minute, thinking about all the things that could go wrong the minute we see Dad again. I don't want to write them down because that might make them actually happen. I know that's probably a ridiculous fear, but any person with anxiety knows that fears are never rational. They're, like, the complete opposite of rational. They're like trying to have a grown-up conversation with the boy next door whose eyes you never noticed were so pretty while your little sister keeps tugging on your arm, asking why she can't go play with her friend down the road even though it's against the rules while Mom's still at work (so is talking to boys . . . or anyone, but let's not get technical) and she's so insistent, she can't take no for an answer, she keeps asking why why why why WHY?

Memaw was trying to make conversation, smooth over the petrified places in her voice. No matter what the circumstances were around Mom and Dad's divorce (and we know them, all right), no matter how much wrong he did (and it was plenty), no matter how much he hurt Mom (and us, too), Mom tries her best not to say a bad word about him. She asked Memaw to do the same, way back at the beginning, but I guess it's easier when Dad is only an abstract part of the equation, not on his way to her house. Still, Memaw was trying. She stuffed another bite of spaghetti in her mouth with a kind of desperate fierceness, like if she could fill her mouth enough, she wouldn't be tempted to say what she really wanted to say.

"Not really." Jack answered the question for all of us.

The truth is, we have no idea. We don't know where Dad's living, what he's been doing these past two years, who—

Nope. Can't think about that. It is off-limits.

"Maybe go fishing?" I let the words fall out so they covered up all the others in my brain, the ones I don't want to—can't—write yet.

Dad took us fishing a few times when we were younger. It never ended well.

"He's taking us school shopping," Maggie threw into the silence that solidified around us, like we were stuck in a pit of quicksand, fast approaching Things We Shouldn't Talk About. Thank goodness for Maggie.

She chewed on the side of her lip, like I'd seen her do a million times before when she was thinking. I don't know her well enough to say whether she was thinking of shoes and shorts and shirts in every shade of her favorite color (I think it's red, but even that's a guess—an educated one, based on her backpack, her folders, and every spiral notebook she needed this year for fourth grade) or just pondering the simple fact of Dad and his mysterious existence. He started disappearing right after she was born, so he's not much more than a stranger to her. Sometimes I wonder if that's made the divorce easier for her.

"Yeah, I heard," Memaw said. "That's nice of him." She didn't sound like she thought it was nice. Her black-brown eyes—the same ones she gave to Mom and me—flicked to my journals and back up to my face. "Will it be just your dad?"

And just like that, we were in the territory of Things We Shouldn't Talk About. The air around us thickened.

"Probably not," Jack mumbled, at the same time I said, "I hope so."

I hope we'll have Dad to ourselves, but he has a new family now—had it before . . .

No, no, no, no, no. Nothing negative. Nothing gloomy. Nothing to ruin this summer and its promise of answers and connection and maybe even, if Jack and Maggie and I can be the right kind of people, repair. (I have it all figured out, don't worry. I call it The No-Fail Plan to Win Dad Back.)

A month is long enough for a miracle.

Memaw said, "Well, y'all just be careful." That's all she said, and I filled in the blanks for her.

Be careful with your hearts. Be careful with what you believe, be careful with the promises you trust, be careful with the imaginations that run away with scenes of happily-ever-after.

Something set fire to my throat, but it was easy enough to swallow.

*T*HE NO–FAIL PLAN TO WIN DAD BACK

*T*he period of one month will be long enough to:

1. Impress Dad with my wit. (He's probably forgotten how funny I am.)
2. Show Dad I'm all grown up. (I don't think he realized our birthdays passed, so he'll be surprised we've gotten so tall; that's what always surprises everyone else, anyway.)
3. Convince Dad to come home.

Three ways I'll do this:

a. Reading books like the fourth volume of Virginia Woolf's diary (it's thick), a poetry collection by William Carlos Williams (it's literary), and Charles Dickens's *Oliver Twist* (it's both thick and literary).

b. Writing, writing, writing. (He's sure to be impressed by how much time I spend practicing my craft.)

c. SMILING! (Dad doesn't like pouty kids, and since I seem to remember he always called me pouty any time I wasn't smiling, this summer is a summer of SMILES!)

July 15, 7:54 p.m.

J tried not to watch the clock, but the ticking was beating all up inside me now. It's like when you're trying
not to hear your brother practicing the trumpet (he's okay,
just not great), so you turn on some music in your room,
but your house is so small all you can hear is *fluurrrp buuur-*
rrntt gleee-ack. Even with the music blasting. Even singing
along to the music. Even with the music blasting and singing along to the music and covering your ears at the same
time. That trumpet wants to be heard.

That's how it was with the clock. It didn't want to let
me forget, and so the endless loop wriggled in my head. *She*
left at four thirty, it takes three hours to get home, she should be
home by now. She should be home by now. She should be home
by now.

She should be home by now she should be home by now she should be home by now . . .

Mom said she'd call when she made it home, but Memaw's phone has been silent for the last twenty-four minutes. Long enough so that if Mom stopped for gas, she would still be home by now. So if she was overcome by an uncontrollable craving for rocky road ice cream (now I want some!) and had to skid into a convenience store, pick up a pint, and eat it right there in the parking lot, she would still be home by now. So if she did both and also spent some time on a public toilet (they're always disgusting, don't even get me started) due to overconsumption, she would still be home by now.

My throat thickened. The spiral expanded.

Maybe she had a blowout like that one time—

Maybe she had a blowout like that one time but unlike that one time she flipped the car—

Maybe she had a blowout like that one time but unlike that one time she flipped the car and crashed through the windshield and now she's lying on the side of the road, dying—

It gets bad fast.

I took a deep breath (which didn't help; it's hard to breathe around boulder implants in the throat). I wrestled my lips into a smile (which didn't help; I probably looked like I was about to dump out my entire bowl of spaghetti, lap it up like my dog, King, and woof for more). I glanced at the cream-colored phone and willed it to ring (which helped a little, but it never really works for long).

Ring. Ring. Ring—

Please God please God please God—

I'll do anything.

You know it's bad when you start bargaining with someone you can't see.

Memaw stood up. "Everybody get enough to eat?"

I looked at my bowl. I'd hardly touched it. I shoved a few more forkfuls into my mouth and stood up too. "I'll do the dishes."

I was desperate for something to do.

Memaw looked at me sideways, like she knew exactly why I offered. Sometimes I think she can read minds. She said, "She'll call. Don't worry." And my mouth filled up with *How do you know?* But I managed to eat the words. They didn't taste nearly as good as the spaghetti.

People always say things like that: Everything will work out, you'll be all right, your mom will figure out a way to buy those school supplies *and* pay rent *and* keep food in the refrigerator (okay, that last one's a trick phrase I use on myself), but how do we ever *know*? Like *know* know. We don't. Anxiety is good at reminding me of that.

So I didn't say anything to Memaw. People don't know

what it's like living with the spiral in my head, and I didn't think Memaw was up for a crash course tonight. I pressed my lips together (then remembered to SMILE!) and carried my bowl to the sink.

This happens all the time: I worry about Mom being a few minutes late. Mom's always late. Mom's always fine. Everything works out in the end.

Except the one time it won't. Which hasn't happened yet—but it *could*.

"She probably forgot to call," Memaw said to my back. "If she hasn't called by eight fifteen, we'll call her."

I nodded and practiced smiling and pretended it was the scalding water (which, yes, I inflicted on myself, but accidentally) that was responsible for the tears in my eyes. Jack and Maggie set their bowls on the counter and turned easily away, unbothered by Mom's not calling. Sometimes I wish I could be more like them. And then I remember: Jack's putrid feet (he should see a doctor) and Maggie's narcolepsy (she doesn't really have narcolepsy, or at least I don't think she does; she just has a habit of taking a morning nap on our closet floor when it's time to get out to the bus stop). I'd rather be me. Most days.

"Maybe you'll want spaghetti later," Memaw said as she bent to put the bowls on the second shelf of her refrigerator, which already had an uncountable number of clear plastic bowls. It was so crowded she had trouble finding room for the spaghetti and spent a whole minute rearranging and shoving other containers farther back, where they'll grow hair and fur. Jack and I used to play a game with all those hairy leftovers. Which One's the Grossest, we called it. I would have laughed at the picture—all those leftovers waiting to be judged—except I remembered what Jack said the last time I asked him if he wanted to play the game. "That's a stupid game," he said, like maybe I was stupid too. It hurt my feelings *way* more than it probably should have.

My chest squeezed tighter.

Growing up doesn't leave much room for fun, I guess.

When Memaw met my eyes, I could tell she meant something else with her words. So *that's* the "later": She doesn't think Dad's going to show up.

I wondered if my chest could get any tighter without killing me. My right arm went numb. I shook it out and jabbed it under the hot water so I could remind myself I wasn't really dying, it was just panic.

I know Dad's not the most reliable person in the world. He's said a lot of things over the years ("I'll call you soon" comes to mind), made all kinds of promises that didn't work out (like, for example, "I do"), shared plans that collapsed as they were coming out of his mouth ("As soon as

I'm done with this job, we'll go to the beach"). But this is different, isn't it? This time he'll follow through.

Won't he?

I didn't need another thing to worry about.

"You know." Memaw looked at me like she knew exactly which hole my thoughts had skidded into, like she knew how slick the sides of that hole were. "You kids are good kids." She put an arm around me. I'm already taller than she is, so she has to look up a little to see into my eyes, which she did. She said the words again: "You kids are good kids." And then she added more: "Anyone who makes you feel otherwise is an ignorant nitwit."

Memaw's creative when it comes to insults. Take a ride with her on the highways of Houston and you'll learn all sorts of new words and phrases.

I started laughing. Memaw started laughing. We laughed until we cried. And when I'd dried all my laughter-tears, I said, "I know."

She was still laughing when she said, "Do you?"

Do I?

July 15, 8:02 p.m.

The phone's shrill ring finally joined the song of the grandfather clock, and my relief was so large, I almost laughed until I cried again.

Phone conversation with Mom, as best I remember:

Me: Hi, Mom.

Mom: Hi, sweetie.

Me: You got home late. Did you have to stop for something?

Mom: I've actually been home for a while. I forgot to call. I'm sorry. Did you worry?

Me: No. (For an hour! While you were forgetting you ever had kids! Already! We've only been gone for an afternoon!)

Mom: Do you have everything you need?

Me: I think so.

Mom: The supplies I gave you?

Me: Moooom!

Mom: I'm just checking. You know it's about time—

Me: Okay, Mom, that's great, everything's fine.

Mom: Memaw can get you more if you need them. Actually, put her on the phone—

Me: No, Mom! I'll be fine.

Mom: Okay, sweetie.

Me: What will you do while we're gone?

Mom: . . . I don't really know.

Me: Read.

Mom: Work.

Me: Sleep.

Mom: Cook for myself, maybe.

Me: You're totally gonna go hungry.

Mom: I'll miss you.

Me: I'll miss you too.

Mom: I love you, Tori.

Me: Call me Victoria.

Mom: Okay, Victoria. Y'all call me when you make it to Ohio.

The whole time we talked, I could see her, leaning her black-curled head against the doorway to the room Maggie and I share, twirling the phone cord around her finger, staring at something outside the kitchen window that she couldn't really see. Her face wasn't a bit blurry. Mom's around all the time. I've never had a chance to forget her.

How long does it take for someone's face to fade into a blur?

Mom had to work tomorrow, or else she'd be here. Or maybe not. Maybe she didn't want to see Dad again—and who could blame her, after what he did?

I'm starting to think gloomy thoughts are harder to chase away after eight p.m. And I still have an hour to go until bedtime. (Mom's bedtime. Memaw doesn't care what time we go to bed.)

This should be fun rereading.

THE PERIOD OF TWO YEARS (AKA WHAT DAD MISSED)

J got contacts and no longer have to wear those ugly purple glasses with the superglued end piece.

I grew six whole inches!

I'm now taller than Jack and feel like an Amazon woman. (He's not very happy about it and refuses to stand right next to me for any sort of documenting purposes.)

Mom let me start wearing clear mascara. (It makes my eyelashes look like I've just taken a swim in the city pool, but at least I get to wear *something*. She says when I get back I might be able to pick out some lip gloss too.)

I wrote two books. (They're not great, but at least I finished them.)

I read too many books to count, including three volumes of Virginia Woolf's diaries, two collections of Emily

Dickinson's poetry, and twelve Victoria Holt mysteries.

I beat Tina Greene in the race to the T. (One-point-eight miles in the blazing heat of the day.)

The Waco siege. (Police and military officers rescued some kids from a compound that belonged to some religious order called the Branch Davidians and lots of people died and it was weird and sad and a national tragedy right here in Texas.)

The murder of Selena, the Mexican American singer who lived in Corpus Christi. (You really don't want to rehash those gruesome details, do you? Also, what is it with Texas? Weird stuff happening here. I bet Dad loves that; he hated Texas and never let Mom forget it.)

I started middle school. (It's not all that different from elementary school, except the boys are a little smaller than the girls, the girls are a little meaner than they were last year, and the building includes locker rooms where you have to shower after athletics class if you don't want to smell like a sweaty sock the rest of the day. I've now perfected my No One Sees Me Naked method of showering.)

I twirled my baton, after months of practice, and made the squad. (It's not a *cheerleading* spot or anything, but yelling hurts my voice and air splits hurt my eyes and would probably hurt my body if I ever tried. Plus, I like the way the silver baton shines and flashes and the breathtaking pain of catching a good toss right across your palm. And someday maybe I'll be one of those fire twirlers, who knows?)

I moved my Sally doll from my bed to my closet at night. (Sometimes she gets scared all by herself, so I move her back to my bed—but not all the time.)

The phone rang and I thought it was him.

The phone rang and I thought it was him.

The phone rang and I finally knew it wasn't him.

I grew up—kind of.

July 15, 11:56 p.m.

I couldn't sleep, so I slipped out of the room where Maggie was sleeping on the bottom bunk, crowding my space, and Jack was snoring on the top bunk.

In the hallway, I folded myself against the white wall, which looked gray in the dim light. From there I could see Memaw hunched over her kitchen table. I couldn't see what she was doing, but I already knew she had a crossword puzzle open in front of her, a bag of Lay's potato chips beside her. She says it keeps her mind sharp, doing so many puzzles late at night and into the early-morning hours. I wonder if maybe she should just get more sleep, since she still forgets where she left her keys and whether she already bought a package of cream horns (which is why she brings at least three when she visits us) and all those leftovers in her fridge.

I opened my notebook and smoothed out a page. I wasn't really sure what to write. I hope I'm not developing writer's block already. I hear it's a terrible, terrible thing. Virginia Woolf complains quite a bit about having the words but not having the will. Maybe that will be me too.

No. It won't. I won't let it be. If you don't have the will, you have to will yourself to have the will. I will will myself to write, even if I say absolutely nothing. There's always tomorrow to say something.

For as long as I can remember, I've kept a journal. Mom used to call me our family recorder because when someone couldn't remember the date of something, all I had to do was pull out my journal. I recorded everything: the day Dad brought home our German shepherd puppy we named Heidi (we haven't seen her in two years, since he kept her with him); the day our blue-eyed kitten, Sugar, braved the Bus Monster and lost and Mrs. Miller, the Bus Monster driver, cried all the way to school, along with Maggie and me; the day Mom took Dad's shotgun and blew rattlesnake guts all over the porch and screen door (she also blew a hole in the screen door, because she wasn't about to venture out onto the porch with a rattlesnake curled up in a corner) and how that dead snake twisted like one of Maggie's hair ribbons caught in a gust of September air, split in two, and slid to rest right in front of the door (but never really rested;

snakes move even after they're dead). She called a neighbor after that (I'm not really sure why, since the hard part was over), and he carried away the dead snake and its rattle on the teeth of a rake. We didn't know what he did with the snake, but Jack and I had our guesses. (I said he probably hollowed it out and stuffed it so he could hang it up like a prize; Jack said he probably ate it. I'm not sure which guess was worse.)

All the details of life, recorded in my composition books.

Mom says my words belong to me until I decide I want to share them—if I ever do. Still, I hide my journals. I don't want any peeking eyes shaped like burnt macadamia nuts (that's Maggie) or coffee-colored almonds (that's Jack). Not even Mom's dark-chocolate-covered pistachios should snoop.

I used to have three rules for my journals:

1. Tell the truth about myself. (Virginia Woolf says, "If you do not tell the truth about yourself you cannot tell it about other people.")
2. Tell the truth about other people. (See above quote.)
3. Tell the truth about what you're feeling and what you experience.

You'll notice they all boil down to one rule, really: Tell the truth. But I realized somewhere in all my writing that even the truth can be slippery. I don't remember things the same way Jack does, because I'm not him. Maggie doesn't remember things the same way I do, because she's not me. So I changed my rules to this one: Tell *my* truth—about myself, about other people, about what I'm feeling and what I experience.

When I was younger, I started every entry with "Dear Diary," like my words belonged to someone invisible, but now I write to someone real: Future Me. What does Future Me need to hear today? What will make her laugh or think or feel warm and gooey inside (which is how happiness feels to me)? What does she need to remember or process through or, maybe, forget so she can successfully live her life? (Writing it down helps let go of those things I need to forget; I just mark those pages with "FORGETTING IN PROCESS. DO NOT REREAD.")

Two years ago a series of entries began with "No phone call from Dad today." Future Me (which is really Present Me) doesn't like to reread those (although I appreciate Past Me recording them), or the ones before that, which report, in wobbly handwriting that's hard to read (okay, I've reread them once): "A letter came today. Aunt Jeanine said Dad has another family that isn't us and a girlfriend even though he's married, and I don't really know what to think because it can't be true, can it?" and, "It's true. Dad has another daughter with his girlfriend, and Mom and Dad are getting a divorce and there's nothing we can do about it and I sort of wish I could die."

Obviously, I didn't die, and I'm glad. And while I appreciate that Past Me survived her dark night of the soul by writing in her journal (which Mrs. Barnes, my sixth-grade English teacher, listed as one of the many benefits of daily journaling), I try to stay away from those pages. Emotions are contagious sometimes.

I've never been the most optimistic person in the world, but I'd like to think this summer will be better than the past two. I'm wearing contacts (well, not right now. I'm not supposed to sleep in them, and I'm supposed to be sleeping), I have journals and a billion story ideas, and Dad's coming.

Dad's coming, and I'll record the whole thing.

I'll arrange whatever pieces come my way.

*M*y eyes stung when I opened them this morning. I didn't get nearly enough sleep, and my body felt achy and heavy. I managed to drag myself out of bed, but it was like peeling the sticker off one of the spaghetti sauce containers Mom likes to keep for storage. (We never use them; they just sit in the cabinet, taking up space, all that peeling and scraping done for nothing.) I think I left parts of myself behind. But the parts I left behind must not weigh anything, because my feet winced on the way to the bathroom.

Maggie and Jack were still sleeping. I was the last one asleep and the first one awake.

Welcome to Victoria's Secret to One-Bathroom-for-Four-People Privileges: Go to bed last, get up first.

I was so heavy I couldn't even laugh at myself. I almost

turned around and climbed back in bed. But it was six thirty, and Dad was supposed to be here in an hour. I had a whole list of things to do:

Shower.

Dress in my best, most grown-up outfit, chosen two weeks ago and laid out yesterday afternoon, to minimize the wrinkles (first impressions are important, especially with the dad you haven't seen in two years).

Put in my contacts (no dorky purple superglued glasses today!).

Brush my teeth (before and after breakfast).

Apply clear mascara in two coats.

Double-check my suitcase to make sure everything's where it should be.

Check again.

And maybe again.

One more time?

Probably another.

Which means if I don't get started now, Dad will show up before I'm ready.

July 16, 8:02 a.m.

*T*he bags wait by the door.

Dad's not here yet.

Writing passes the time.

This is an account of Our Last Breakfast.

Jack and Maggie eventually joined Memaw and me at her kitchen table. A mostly eaten bowl of Shredded Wheat (with a few soggy leftovers) sat in front of me for about twelve minutes, Raisin Bran in front of Maggie and Jack (Jack's second bowl—I don't know how he can still eat), and nothing in front of Memaw, because she's not a breakfast person, unless that breakfast includes jelly-filled donuts, a Hostess fried apple pie, or a cream horn. She didn't have any of those in stock today. It's like Mom was here, cleaning out her kitchen. (I wouldn't put it past her;

Mom's always telling Memaw she needs to take better care of herself.)

"Everybody sleep well?" Memaw said. She was trying to lift the silence at the table. It was almost as heavy as I was when I got out of bed this morning.

"Not really," I said, at the same time Jack said, "About as well as can be expected."

Memaw grimaced and looked like she wanted to say something, but Maggie beat her to it. "I slept fine," she said. She wasn't concerned at all about what would happen in . . . (I looked at the clock) . . . four more minutes, if Dad wasn't late.

"You been working on any stories, Tori?" Memaw was really trying hard to distract us. Jack's leg bounced under the table.

My chest felt warm when I said, "A couple."

Memaw raised her eyebrows. "About . . . ?"

I'm not one for sharing my secrets before the stories are done, so I said, "I'm not really sure yet, but as soon as I write them, I'll let you know."

Memaw's eyes shone. She looked at Jack and then Maggie. "You have everything you need?" Her eyes flicked back to me.

We all nodded. The clock ticked on. 7:31.

"You sure?" Memaw said. "I have extras if you need them."

I wondered if she bought the extras because we were coming or if she just has them stacked around in her product-filled room.

I've already double- and triple- and quadruple-checked my suitcase. Actually, I lost count of how many times I checked to make sure I had everything, including the Womanhood Supplies Mom made me bring.

That was an embarrassing conversation. Mom said I'm getting older, and it's possible that I might be visited by a special visitor while I'm in Ohio, which made the whole thing sound creepy and weird, and so I told her I'd already had this educational "talk" in fifth grade, when we all watched some cheesy video that I can't remember much about except for how hot my cheeks felt—hotter than the afternoon asphalt in mid-August would be a pretty good estimate—and had some quick class discussion after the video, so I was probably good on the details, we didn't need to go over them again, and Mom said you can't be too prepared and I said maybe you *can* be too prepared, it's okay not to do this again, and she shoved the Womanhood Supplies into my suitcase, right at the top, for all the world to see. I buried them under my pajamas.

(And that, my dear Future Me, is a grand example of a run-on sentence (the middle one between the two short ones in the paragraph above), used to convey mortification, in this case. But you probably already know that because you're a writer now.)

My cheeks flamed again, just thinking about that conversation with Mom and the supplies that always seem to float to the top of my suitcase, no matter how deep I bury them.

Memaw was not giving up. "Toothbrushes? Toothpaste? Underwear?"

Wait.

Jack snickered.

"You have extra underwear in your room?" I said. "In our size?"

Jack laughed out loud. It sure was good to hear that again. It's not that he'd ever stopped laughing completely, but he did forget how for a while.

Memaw laughed too. "Depends on what size you wear," she said.

I had no idea if she was serious, but I would not be surprised.

More minutes passed.

I thought maybe Memaw's clock was a little fast.

Or maybe he was just late. People can be late. Mom's always late.

Or maybe he wasn't showing up.

"Did you pack any games?" Memaw looked at Maggie.

Maggie's favorite game is Clue, and the only time we get to play it is here at Memaw's.

Maggie shook her head.

"Want to pack one?" Memaw said.

"I don't think we have room." I don't know why I answered for Maggie. I annoy even myself.

Maggie shot me a Maggie Look, which is something between irritated, angry, offended, and, if possible, unconcerned. (She's a roll-with-the-punches sort of person, whereas I'm a try-to-redirect-the-punches-even-if-you're-completely-powerless kind of person.)

"Your dad can carry one extra bag," Memaw said, and she got up, disappeared into her bedroom, and returned to the table with a canvas bag that said, "A woman needs a man like a whale needs a book."

Dad's gonna love that one. I bet she had it specially made.

We followed Memaw to the room where we slept. She rummaged in the closet until she found Clue and slid it into the bag, along with Uno and SkipBo and the Game of Life. She leaned the bag against our suitcases and glanced toward the door.

It was almost eight.

"I knew he'd be late," Memaw said. Then she cleared her throat like she hadn't meant to say the words out loud.

She smiled in our direction, but it was so tight it looked like it might snap.

Maybe he's not coming.

I will NOT let that voice win. He *will* show up, if only by force of my will (and we know how strong that can be. See last night's "I don't know what to write" entry).

And then I heard it: the unmistakable sound of a car pulling into the drive. Memaw's shoulders slumped all the way to the floor.

Should I be worried that she looked worried instead of relieved?

*T*he doorbell rang. My throat was so dry it clicked when I swallowed.

Don't be weird, don't be weird, don't be weird.

"Do you think he'll like us?" The question was an accidental blurt. Jack smacked my shoulder like I said something stupid, which, of course, I did.

Memaw gave me a strange look. "He's your dad. He's supposed to love you just because you're his kids."

Jack opened the door before I could say another stupid thing, before I was even ready, before I had a chance to look at myself in a mirror and make sure I didn't have any Frosted Mini Wheats crumbs sticking to my cheeks or crammed between my teeth. I didn't even have the chance to use the bathroom, and that knowledge, along with the one thousand two hundred miles we'd be traveling with a man who doesn't like taking bathroom breaks, sent me running for the bathroom.

Words from the past chased me.

Wipe that pout off your face before you trip on your lip. Stand up straight unless you want to be a hunchback like your nana. You don't need seconds, you've had more than enough.

I shook them off as best I could and told myself that this summer would be different because *I'm* different: I smile (he won't be able to tell what's fake and what's real, anyway), I stand up straight (when I remember), I try not to eat too much (as long as it's not pizza. Or ice cream. Or hamburgers. Or . . . well, I'll try not to eat seconds while I'm visiting).

Before opening the bathroom door, I plastered a gigantic smile on my face. It was so big, I could feel it touching my ears.

Dad stood at the front door, waiting. He has the same green eyes, the same long lashes that curl around them like they do mine, the same smile that settles into those eyes long after his lips have moved on to other things, like he's amused by the whole world. He has the same black hair (it's thinned a little, but I'll never point that out to him), the same long legs (he's not quite as tall as I remember, but maybe that's just because I'm an Amazon-girl-woman now), the same strong arms covered in such thick hair that it once embarrassed me when we went to a water park and he took off his shirt and I wondered if he was wearing the skin of a chimpanzee. (It's not really that bad. It was just . . . shocking.)

"Wondered when you'd be done, Tori," Dad said. "Always the last one in the bathroom, aren't you?"

I couldn't tell if he was joking or if he meant the words as an insult. I decided to go with joking.

But how did I forget this, the confusion between ha ha that's funny and pay attention so you can be someone different?

I glanced at Memaw. She narrowed her eyes at Dad.

But before she could say anything, Dad said, "Go on and get in the car. Plenty of room for everyone."

I should have known he wasn't just talking about me and Jack and Maggie.

Maybe I didn't prepare myself well enough. Maybe I should have envisioned that moment, the moment when I would look at his car (it's a Suburban, rusted gray, all its windows rolled down) and see a woman with long, straight hair so red it's orange (that is not a natural color), one pale arm hanging out the passenger-side window, and a little girl with enormous green eyes and white-blond hair staring at us from the second row of seats. Maybe I should have known, but I didn't let myself know.

And now there is a cat—no, a cougar—tearing at my chest, still, twenty minutes after I first saw them.

I didn't know they were coming.

Memaw stood at my elbow, tight-lipped and stiff. Her grumble was so soft I almost didn't hear it. "He said he wouldn't bring them." Her eyes seemed to say the rest of everything she couldn't.

Dad finished putting our bags in the back of the Suburban. "Good to see you, Nora," he said, lifting a hand in something that might be called a Weak Wave, if one were in the business of naming things. Memaw returned his Weak Wave with a Weaker Wave and added more insincere words to the others already floating above us, in real danger of disintegrating from either the steamy summer humidity or the steamy hate boiling between the two of them: "Good to see you too, Jerry."

Yeah, right.

"Get in the car, kids," Dad said, ducking into the driver's seat. The engine clattered. Memaw turned me toward her and folded me in her arms.

"You call me if you need anything," she said, and I nodded against her chest, the words rumbling through my head. My nose burned. I didn't want to cry, but how does a person *not* cry during moments of goodbye to the ones they love and hello to the ones they . . . don't know?

All I knew was I couldn't let Dad see me cry. He never liked it when we cried. I remember that. I remember a lot of things that I don't want to write down yet. Maybe never.

Memaw pulled away and stood looking at me for a second before saying, "Don't be anyone other than your-self, you hear me, Tori? You can't be someone different just because it's easier for a person. Doesn't do any good. Can't change who you are without losing yourself." She glared toward Dad and said the same thing she'd said inside the house. "He should love you just because you're his kids."

Then Memaw hugged Jack and Maggie too. I tried to swallow the Stonehenge-size boulder in my throat, but it came right back, made of a red-haired woman, a green-eyed girl, and—was that a baby seat I saw in the car?

Yes. Yes it was.

Another boulder made of one word: Replaced.

"I'll miss you," Memaw called as I followed Jack and Maggie toward the rusty Suburban.

"I'll miss you too," I called back over my shoulder. My voice felt wobbly and thick, like that boulder was making more boulders, pressing on more than just my throat.

I moved around to the other side of the Suburban but didn't make it all the way. For a second I stood behind it, staring at the backs of their heads.

A girl, a woman, my dad, and a baby strapped in a baby seat.

Plenty of room for everyone, or plenty of room for The Replacements?

I climbed into the third row of seats, where Jack sat at the other window and Maggie slid to the middle, not complaining about her seat assignment for maybe the first time ever.

Memaw watched as we pulled away. I shifted in my seat so I could see her until she turned tiny and disappeared, looking like a lone oak in a forest of pines.

I felt about the same way.

CHAMELEON: A GLOOMY-ISH REFLECTION

A chameleon changes colors
depending on the environment

A chameleon changes personalities
depending on the audience

A chameleon changes preferences
depending on the activity at hand

A chameleon changes likes and dislikes
depending on the stakes

A chameleon pays attention, assesses danger,
and adapts to stay alive

This summer I will be
a chameleon

(And I'll try really hard
not to lose my tail)

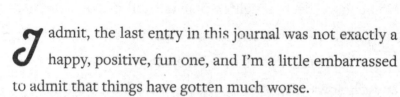

I admit, the last entry in this journal was not exactly a happy, positive, fun one, and I'm a little embarrassed to admit that things have gotten much worse.

(But first, a side note: Did you know that chameleons don't regrow their tails if they lose theirs? That's the point of my last line. But I guess if a poet has to explain her poetic choices, they kinda lose their power.)

Jack is sweating more than I've ever seen him sweat (and you should have seen his athletics shirt after football two-a-days last week). He wipes at his forehead every few minutes, but that's not helping anything. Where do you wipe the sweat you wipe when you're already soaking wet? My back is so sweat-soaked, I had to lean forward in a frog-like position (my legs are so long my knees are almost poking my eyeballs) in hopes that maybe it will air out a little. Even Maggie has a sparkling film on her face, and Maggie will complain about being cold in three-digit-degree weather. I know this because two weeks ago, when I asked her to ride bikes with me outside, she took one step out onto our sagging, holey porch, and said, "I think I'll wait until it's a little warmer." It was already one hundred and one degrees.

There's a reason it's so hot in this car.

What happened is the little girl, Anna, complained about the wind blowing her hair in her face (an easy fix would have been a tighter ponytail, or maybe a French braid, or maybe even chopping all her hair off), so Dad told Jack and me to help roll up all the windows. We don't have any windows where we're sitting in the Way Back (which is why the Back Sweat Salt Lake started in the first place—now it's an ocean), so we had to unbuckle our seat belts and lean over the middle seat to roll up the windows there. It took me a while to get my side up, and the entire terrifying time I rolled, I saw visions of Dad's Suburban colliding with another car, crinkling up, ejecting me through the window like a cartwheeling cheerleader who spent years in gymnastics but never learned how to land on her feet. I saw myself, twisted and mangled on the side of the road somewhere in East Texas. I saw Dad shrug and say, "You win some, you lose some."

Well, okay, that last part wasn't in my original vision. I imagined it after I was back where I was supposed to be, the seat belt tugged tight around me, one hand on the back of the seat, to steady myself. Maybe it's inaccurate and even a little unfair, or, dare I say it, unreasonable to imagine something so harsh coming from Dad's mouth, but really: risk two of his kids' lives for the comfort of one? That doesn't sound very wise. Or rational. Or fatherly.

I'm really trying not to glare at the back of Anna's head. Dad can see me from the rearview mirror, so I smile like I am the happiest person on earth. I am so happy rolling up the windows for one of The Replacements. I am so happy sitting in this sweltering car and feeling the sweat trickle down every crack I have. I am so happy to be trapped here for another fourteen hours, minus stops (which means many, many more hours with a baby and a three-year-old).

I have to admit, flying through the windshield and cartwheeling through the air only to face-plant into the dried-up straw they call grass somewhere in East Texas probably would have been a preferable death to this suffocating one. I keep taking deep breaths and immediately regretting it.

Jack must have forgotten to put on deodorant today. At first I thought maybe it was me, so I lifted my right arm a little and sniffed. Lavender and rose, but fading fast. I can't remember if I packed my deodorant in a pocket or somewhere under all my clothes, or, God forbid, beneath my Womanhood Supplies. Either way, I doubt Dad would let me get it.

I'm still not used to this body-changing thing. Hair, sweat, things growing that have no business growing (and others that I want to grow, please grow, please, please, please), a looming date with The Visitor one of these days (but hopefully never and most definitely not in the next thirty days).

"Can you open your window, Tori?" Maggie leaned over and said a few minutes ago, distracting me from my strange and private thoughts, and I was glad. She pressed a hand against the window beside me.

"These don't open," I said, and pushed her back to her spot. Except we stuck together. She peeled half my skin off when she went.

A dull ache started then, right behind my eyes.

Just what I needed: a headache on top of everything else. Headaches make it much more difficult to smile.

I felt Dad's eyes on me, so I pasted on my best grin. I am a grinning fool. Joker without the scars, a plastic Barbie without the body or the perfect hair or the blue eyes or the cool clothes. Okay, I'm nothing like Barbie.

"It's so hot," Maggie whispered. She can be persistent when she wants to be. Now was not the time.

"I know," I said, trying my best to soothe her. "Maybe we'll stop soon." Stopping would mean getting a good look at The Replacements, but it would also mean fresh air.

Dad caught my eye in the rearview mirror. His eyes crinkled up, and he said, "Man, you kids sweat a lot. I can see you shining all the way up here." Like there was anything we could do about that, with the windows closed up tight. He was smiling, so I couldn't tell if this was Friendly Teasing Dad or Demeaning Dad.

I forgot there were two. More than two. Many, many different Dads. And we'll probably see them all this summer, if we're the opposite of lucky.

I wonder how you forget things like this, things that used to make you kind of glad for the days you came home from school and your mom said, "Your dad's gone out of town for another job. He'll be back in a couple of months." You missed him, of course, but only the idea of him. I guess that's what happens when you mix time with absence: You construct your own version of who your dad is and try to reconcile the imagined with the real when they meet.

This is getting philosophical. I must be in a hallucinatory state brought on by extreme heatstroke.

The baby strapped in the carrier beside Anna started fussing, little sounds that reminded me of the squeaky toys we used to give our old dog, Heidi, for Christmas. Lisa, in the front seat, turned around and stuck a pacifier in his mouth. (Dad didn't introduce us, by the way. I just heard him say her name earlier. I guess he didn't feel the need to introduce his old family to his new one.) The baby spit it out, and his sounds got louder and louder, until they could accurately be called a wail. Just what we all wanted to add to this sweaty car and my aching head: a wailing baby. "He's hungry," Lisa said to Dad.

"Well, we'll stop in a little while," Dad said. He didn't sound very happy about this, and I couldn't help the lightning-fast streak of satisfaction that shot through my chest.

I'm a terrible person, I know.

"You kids hungry?" Dad said, eyeing us again in the rear-view mirror. It felt like a trick question. It was past noon, past our normal lunchtime, but if we said we were hungry, did that mean we were complaining? If there's one thing I remember about Dad (and as the minutes tick by, there are plenty more), it's that he *really* doesn't like complaining.

I was still trying to figure out how to outsmart Dad at his own game when Jack said, "Whatever."

I thought it was brilliant, at least until Dad said, "What kind of punk answer is that? You're either hungry or you're not." He shook his head. "Whatever. You kids."

You kids. Like we're not even his.

My chest blazed, and I rubbed it hard. Good thoughts, good thoughts, only good thoughts allowed here, I reminded myself.

I said, "We'll eat if we stop."

"Yeah, I bet you will," Dad said. "I remember how much you love to eat."

I swallowed hard, looked out the window, watched the fields pass, and tried not to let his words sink into the soft places of my body (but there are so many). Those places where I've begun to wonder if I *am* a little *too* un-Barbie-like.

The baby (I can't remember his name, I'm sorry) cried louder, like he could hear all the words bottled up inside me, clawing to get out.

If I wrote them, if I let them spill onto these pages, I would not have enough journals to contain them. So I only write a few:

This was a terrible, terrible idea.

I want to go back home.

Would hitchhiking be a good escape plan?

(Absolutely, positively not. I would never get into a car with a person I don't know. Even if they offered me an end-less supply of Trolli Sour Brite Crawlers and had a whole back seat full of the value-size packages to prove they could keep me snacking on them for years. Well, I'd have to give it some serious thought. But no. Maybe. No.)

July 16, 3:07 p.m.

*T*he baby quieted down and went to sleep, so Dad kept driving. Maybe it was a mistake not to admit that we were hungry. Just when I was thinking this, Jack's stomach gave a big empty howl, and Maggie started laughing, which made me laugh, which made Jack laugh.

"Something funny back there?" Dad said. He wants to know everything, but I don't think it's real interest. It's like he wants to make sure we're laughing at the *right* thing. Is it control, concern, or something else?

I remember this: the eggshells, the careful way we had to justify ourselves, the feeling that you never know what you'll get when you open your mouth to say something. Will you be understood or misjudged? Will he laugh, or will he yell? Will you want to cry (but blink really hard so you don't), or will you feel a giant whoosh of relief?

Dad's question twirled in what little wind we could feel in the Way Back. I don't think any of us knew how to answer it.

Jack decided to solve the problem with "Maggie farted, and it vibrated the whole seat."

Then we really *did* laugh. Jack's not one for making up stories, but that one—well, it was a good one. Even Dad loves a good fart joke.

Lisa apparently doesn't. Her eyes were hard when she turned to look at us from the front seat, but she didn't say anything. In the rearview mirror, I saw Dad's eyes crinkle, and even though I couldn't see if the smile actually reached his mouth, I knew he was as amused as we were. It felt like a victory.

I returned to staring out my window. Jack returned to staring out his, and Maggie stared at her lap, fidgeting with her fingers. She didn't bring anything to do on the trip, and for a minute I felt sorry for her.

Jack has his Stephen King books, which are not at all appropriate for a nine-year-old of Maggie's maturity level. (I don't even like to read them. My imagination is terrifying enough, thank you.) I have my notebooks.

I figured I could share.

I slipped Maggie one of them without saying anything. She opened it to the first page. I'd already written on it, so I said, "Just don't read anything." She nodded and flipped through to a fresh page, but instead of drawing or writing, she just doodled her name. Maggie Reeves. Maggie Reeves. Maggie Reeves, over and over again. Was she trying to remember who she was? Had she already forgotten, less than seven hours after starting The First Magnificent Summer with Dad?

My throat tightened as I stared at her doodles. I guess I felt a little protective of Maggie. And Jack, too. It's us against the world. Us against The Replacements. Us against . . .

Dad.

Maggie whispered, "How far is it to Cleveland?"

"A long way," I said. Maggie sighed. I glanced at Dad in the mirror, but his eyes were on the road. I said, "Just keep yourself distracted." If it weren't so hot in this car, we could all sleep, and the time would melt away just like we were. (Well, I wouldn't sleep. If I'm not watching the road, how will we ever make it safely? I know how ridiculous that sounds, but have you met my mind?)

After a while, Maggie's head started bobbing. I sank down in my seat and eased her head toward my shoulder, knowing I'd have another Sweat Lake or maybe even a Sweat Ocean before we stopped, but she's my little sister, and this is what big sisters do. I slid the notebook out of her hand. She only used one page, writing her name in every tiny space. I guess she knows how precious these pages are to me.

I turned my face to the window and tried to distract myself with rolling waves of dead grass. It was the bleakest kind of landscape you could hope to find on a long and torturous trip. We weren't even out of Texas yet. It's the state that never ends.

Maggie woke up not even an hour after she drifted off. She had to go to the bathroom so badly she started bounc ing in the seat, her legs keeping some imaginary time. Dad looked in the rearview every few minutes, his eyes hardening more and more as time ticked by. I tried not to meet his gaze. I knew if I did, I'd somehow feel like it was my fault.

Another thing I remember.

To tell the truth, I had to go too. Badly. And my head no longer cuddled a dull ache but was home to a construction worker trying to tear up concrete with a sledgehammer.

Twice Maggie almost asked Dad if we could stop, but Jack and I shushed her. She probably doesn't remember the trips we used to take on the way to Memaw's, when Dad would yell about too many stops and this is taking forever and kids should be able to make it two hundred miles down the road without whining about peeing. We'd gone more than two hundred miles, but still. Better safe than sorry. I could tell by Dad's hard eyes and the set of his jaw that we hadn't gone far enough.

Maggie bounced. I gave her a Look. She whispered, "I need to go so bad!"

"We'll stop soon," I whispered back. We still hadn't eaten lunch.

But it wasn't until half an hour later, when Anna announced, "I need to go potty," that Dad pulled off the highway, into a rest area that magically appeared like it heard the golden child speak of her need too.

Maybe Dad always planned on stopping here. Or maybe the game really was stacked against us. Maybe the way kids remember their dads during a long separation is completely different from the way a dad remembers his kids (if he remembers them at all). Maybe Dad only remembers the things he didn't like about us. Maybe he forgot all the good parts.

Well, we have thirty whole days to show him the good parts. Starting with The Always-Present Smile.

I plastered my smile on my face again.

It was past two when we pulled into the rest area.

"May as well eat now," Dad said as he swung into a spot. I could hardly wait to get out of the stifling, sweaty, smelly car, but of course we had to wait for Anna to climb out and for Lisa to unstrap the baby. (I still can't remember his name; I'm hoping they'll say it again so I can write it down this time.) There wasn't a dry spot on my shirt by the time I climbed out, careful not to trip on the seat lever. (That would be a humiliating show of clumsiness, and I am NOT clumsy. Most of the time.) Jack's shirt was even worse. I think you could actually wring a lake out of his. Or at least a small pool.

Poor Jack. He's going through the same thing I'm going through—that is, The Thing that Cannot Be Named but starts with a *P*—but we can't even talk about it.

"Hope you wiped your butt sweat off the seat before you got out," Dad said, his eyes glinting at Jack, his mouth turned up into another one of those not-so-nice smiles. Jack looked behind him like he was trying to figure out if Dad was being serious. He glanced at me. I gave a tiny little shake of my head, which I hoped Jack would interpret as meaning, *He's just kidding*.

Jack's never been all that great at figuring out when someone's joking or not.

Before Jack could say or do anything, Dad said, "Get the cooler out of the back, Jack. I'll go find us a table."

The cooler sat underneath all our luggage, so I helped Jack take out the suitcases, lift out the cooler, and pack the suitcases back inside the space. But when I tried to help Jack carry the cooler to the table, where Dad sat waiting alone, he jerked it away from me and said, "I got it."

I watched him lumber away, carrying something he didn't really have to carry alone.

He forgot to close the back of the Suburban, so I did that, then followed him to the table and got there just in time to hear Dad say, "Carrying the cooler all by yourself, Jack? You sure have gotten strong." His eyes shone as he patted Jack on the back and took the cooler from my brother's hands, set it on the cement slab, and popped it open.

Jack turned away, but not before I saw his smile and all the things swimming in it: satisfaction, glee, and the kind of hunger that squeezed my chest.

No food would fill that hunger.

Not even three double bacon cheeseburgers, which is easily the greasiest burger on Sonic's menu (because bacon) and also, according to Jack, the best (because bacon). Here's a secret I don't tell many people, for obvious The World's Full of Bacon Lovers reasons: I don't like bacon. In fact, I hate it almost as much as I hate bologna, which . . .

Oh, no.

Dad tossed me a plastic sandwich bag. I almost gagged when I saw what was in it.

I should have known. But like I said before, memory's faulty. It forgets things on purpose—like bologna slices smashed between two pieces of white bread smeared with mayonnaise, the official Lunch of Ohio Jack, Victoria, and Maggie.

When I took my first bite, I really did gag, but at least I had the forethought to turn away before Dad saw me.

NOTES ON GROWING UP

*M*om says kids always want to grow up, but then once they do they spend the rest of their lives wanting to be kids again. I don't know about that, because I'm not all the way grown up yet (I know, it's so shocking, considering my maturity), but I do know that growing up doesn't come without its disappointments.

Jack and I used to be like two Skechers sneakers (okay, probably the off-brand kind, since those things are expensive)—one left, one right, but both belonging to the same person. Now I don't really know him anymore. I can't tell if he's been tied too long around a stinky foot or if the sock inside him is too scratchy or if the foot doesn't have a sock at all (ew), and that's what got him all bent out of shape and too big for me.

Or maybe I got too small for him.

I try to imagine what it's like to be Jack, but, well . . . I guess once you hit a certain point, that stops feeling easy, because he's all *Super Mario 64* and *The Simpsons* (tell me how Mom approved that and not *Friends*???) and girls, and you're all Virginia Woolf (and Victoria Holt and Scott O'Dell and Shel Silverstein and Christopher Paul Curtis and Mary Downing Hahn and Madeleine L'Engle and Maya Angelou and Toni Morrison and Lois Lowry and oh! So many! I could go on and on!) and writing and boys (even though you pretend you're not interested because you're not sure anyone would like you and sometimes it's just easier not to hope), and one day you will stand next to him and you're taller than him and he's mad about that but there's nothing you can do—you'd make yourself smaller, you really would, not even the contained world of middle school likes an Amazon-woman-child who takes up space—and you notice then that you're not two Skechers on the same person's feet (you probably never were), but you're still a Skechers sneaker and he's now a Doc Martens, and the feet you're strapped to are walking in opposite directions.

Sometimes growing up also feels like losing. I wonder what Mom would say about that.

July 16, 7:37 p.m.

You don't like bologna?" Dad said, turning his light-saber-green eyes on me. We stopped for supper at another rest stop and had the same thing we had for lunch.

The sides of Dad's mouth twitched, like he had something else he wanted to say, but he was trying really hard not to.

I think bologna tastes like the kind of meat that's photocopied onto a flimsy piece of beef-and-maybe-a-little-pork-flavored plastic and placed between two slices of bread and a liter of mustard just to make it palatable (and I hear it's made from organs and other nasty things, so no, thanks, I'll pass). But of course I was not about to say that.

Instead, I said, "I'm not really hungry," and took a sip of

the grape soda in front of me. A dainty sip. The kind of sip that says, "I am a lady and all grown up."

My stomach, in reality, felt like it could eat a package or two of shells and cheese (the off-brand kind Mom keeps stocked in the pantry would be just fine), a pound of fish sticks, and maybe twelve pickles. And an entire package of Little Debbie's Fudge Rolls, Oatmeal Creme Pies, and Star Crunch. Yes, all three. I don't know what's gotten into me.

I was hungry. But not for bologna. Slapped between airy white bread. (It doesn't even feel like you're eating anything. You're munching on a cloud, nothing more.) And slathered with mayonnaise or, worse, Miracle Whip.

"I guess your mom tolerates picky eaters," Dad said. It wasn't a question. He didn't even wait for a response (and I was glad, because I could feel an eye-rolling coming on, and that was probably the worst possible thing I could do in that situation). He just said, "Here you'll be a hungry little girl if you're picky. Sissy knows that." He lifted a hand and ruffled Anna's hair so it hung in her eyes. She giggled. Lisa smiled. I saw all this from the corners of my eyes, since I wasn't looking at them. I didn't even want to acknowledge their presence.

They weren't supposed to be here.

I wasn't sure if Dad was calling *me* a little girl, or if he'd only said it because he was talking about Anna in an indirect way. And also me. I don't know, I'm confused.

Jack threw me a dirty look, like I was the one in the wrong here. He doesn't like bologna either, but he'd already eaten half his sandwich. I guess some of us are better at pretending than others.

Well, if it was a contest . . .

I slapped a big smile on my face and said, "I'll probably be hungry later," and shoved my sandwich back in its plastic bag.

"Lisa was up at four in the morning making all this food for you kids," Dad said, resting a hand on Lisa's bare thigh.

Well, I was certainly not going to eat it, then. He ruined the whole experience for me. I shoved two chips in my mouth, while Dad's eyes locked on Lisa, so I didn't have to smile or say anything.

"Thank you, Lisa," Jack said, and then it was my turn to throw him a dirty look. Maggie echoed Jack's words. I waited until I'd chewed the chips and swallowed the shards, which scraped all the way down my throat—or maybe it was the words I now had to say because of Jack and Maggie—before I said, "Thank you, Lisa," the ever-dutiful child.

Dad's eyes burned my face, like he was trying to figure out whether I was being sarcastic or genuine, but I didn't give him the satisfaction of seeing the truth in my eyes. (I'm an open book.) The ground was a safer resting place for eyes, so I kept mine there. My smile was still fixed in place, if a little rickety and worn by that point.

Dad slid the bag of Jones' Potato Chips, one of the few things I missed about our year in Ohio, toward me. "Maybe you're hungry for more chips," he said.

The chips are made in Ohio, so we had them all the time the year we lived there. In our Before Divorce life, when Dad was around, he had the chips shipped to Texas, he loves them so much.

And they really are good. My mouth watered just looking at that open bag. The wind flung their smell of salt and grease and crinkle-cut potato toward me, and I swear my stomach gnawed on one side of itself.

Of course I wanted more. I only had three chips left in my kid-sized portion.

But I knew it was a trap.

I decided I'd rather go hungry than be criticized, so I declined. My stomach hates me.

Well, I still had three potato chips left in the sandwich bag Lisa packed. When Dad wasn't looking, I stuffed them in my mouth like a ravenous raccoon (but much less messy).

They didn't taste nearly as good as I remember.

Also, my stomach still hates me.

July 16, 11:57 p.m.

*T*his road is endless, incessant, interminable. All those words mean relatively the same thing, but, in my opinion, refer to the never-ending in varying degrees, interminable being the most intolerable. When you're stuck in a car dying of heatstroke, you have time to think about these things. I wish I could use the opportunity to write my novel in progress, but, honestly, I only have enough energy right now to write in this journal—and barely that. Plus, Dad won't let us turn on a light (he yelled at Jack for trying earlier), because The Replacement Kids are finally sleeping. I'm using the headlights from the cars behind us, but I'm mostly guessing where lines are. (You might not even be able to read this, and, I hate to say it, maybe that will be for the best.)

It's been dark for hours, but I can't sleep. Maggie's head rolled onto my shoulder back around 8:45, when the sun faintly waved its last golden fingers at us and retired for the night. I never realized Maggie had such a heavy head.

Here are the things that have happened since my last entry at 7:37:

Devon cried for an entire hour. (Devon is the baby's name. I forgot to write it down when I heard someone say it, but at least I didn't forget it again!) Lisa said he was hungry.

Welcome to the club.

Dad told Anna to give Devon his binky, we weren't stopping again. Then they played a game called Give Devon His Binky So He Can Spit It Out and Cry Louder for the next twenty minutes or so.

Lisa and Dad argued in the front seat for at least fifteen minutes, while Dad said maybe Devon should be on a feeding schedule and Lisa said maybe he should just stop so she could feed him real quick, and on and on and on it went until I couldn't even take pleasure in the tension between them.

Dad said maybe one of the older kids could feed Devon, if Lisa prepared a bottle.

I thought, *Absolutely not.*

Lisa said, "Absolutely not."

Dad stopped.

This happened three times.

Dad said we'd be to Grandma's by two a.m., if we didn't have any more stops. That was two stops ago.

Maggie asked me "How much longer?" 4,012 times, and I repeated "I have no idea" an equal number of times.

And last, but definitely not least, the final beads of the entire measure of my sense of humor sweated out of me at mile one thousand and one.

Now we sit and wait. My butt has a cramp so bad, I might not be able to walk once we get to Grandma's. Every now and then my back pulses with the kind of throb that slams into you and takes your whole breath with it. Everything aches.

How much longer? I have no idea.

Maggie flinched awake about twenty minutes ago. "How much longer?" she whispered.

I glanced at the dashboard and pulled her head back down to my shoulder. "Just go back to sleep," I said. My eyes felt heavy enough to close, and I almost let them. But there was the matter of the journal. I couldn't leave it unattended, not when it was so visible. Not when it has so much about . . . well, you know.

At home, I either hide whatever journal I'm using under my pillow (that's for the nighttime), or I carry it with me at all times. I won't say where I hide all the finished ones, because if you're Future Me, you already know, and if you're not Future Me, you shouldn't be reading this in the first place. Unused journals I keep in my sock drawer. I always try to have at least four blank journals waiting for me. You never know when you'll have the kind of brilliant inspiration that fills an entire journal, and then another and another. It hasn't happened yet, but at least I'm prepared.

I am *way* off topic.

Jack's still awake. He's been staring out the window since Dad yelled at him for trying to turn on a light, which was around ten thirty. Every now and then I try to catch his eye, let him know I'm totally on his side, but he seems determined not to look at anyone, even more so than usual.

Nothing outside the window looks familiar. I feel too far away from home. And Mom. And Memaw.

I try not to think about this, because of what Dad said a few minutes ago.

"Is my little girl pouting back there?" he said. I caught his eye in the mirror, thinking he couldn't possibly be talking about me, since I'm not a little girl and also, I'm not really his. Not anymore. But Anna was still asleep. "The trip too long for you?"

I guess I let my smile slip off my face (or maybe it melted off). I carved it back into my cheeks and said, "I love long road trips. So much to see," without even the tiniest piece of sarcasm. I was extra proud of myself.

Dad still bristled, like he's primed to take offense at whatever I say. Three cars whirred by as we passed them. I don't think Dad can possibly go one speed—one minute he's passing all the cars, the next minute they're passing him.

"Why are you pouting, then?" he said. You'd think he'd want it as quiet as possible here in the car, since everyone but Jack and me and maybe Lisa were—are—sleeping.

"I'm not pouting," I said, loud enough for Dad to hear me, even though I risked all kinds of things with my arguing. But my voice broke, the traitor.

Anna's head popped up just as Dad said, "Your mama probably lets you kids walk around pouting about everything. Getting your way all the time." I stared at Dad in the mirror, but he kept his eyes fixed on the road. I was glad, because I'm not sure how many daggers flew out of mine and into the back of his head. Maybe seven? More? He continued, like I hadn't already gotten his point: smile more. "I won't tolerate that kind of crap this summer."

Dictation note required here: He didn't say "crap," but I'm not allowed to write bad words, and even though this journal is my private possession and I can write whatever I want, I choose not to use bad words. I think they're unnecessary for getting your point across. For example: I knew

Dad was mad. I could see it (1) in his eyes, (2) in the way his shoulders tightened up, (3) in the line of his lips, and (4) in the fierce tone of his words. No need for swearing.

Dad said more stuff, but I walled off my ears, because it was the kind of stuff that used to make me cry when I was a little girl, and maybe I'm not quite as old and mature as I thought I was before I started this trip. Maybe I'm still Tori, not Victoria.

I'm not proud to say that some of his words got all tangled up in my throat, like they were made of stone and mortar and a tiny little stonemason who wants to build a wall right in front of my tonsils. I coughed, tried to loosen up what was stuck, but it remains. Stubborn, like I used to be before I encountered this road trip.

Now I feel soft.

Anna interrupted Dad to say she was hungry, and Lisa told her we'd be at Grandma's soon; thank you for not whining and pouting. I heard in her words more than she said: *Thank you for being better than them.*

I still had a few daggers left. I aimed them at the back of her head.

And now, because I can think of absolutely nothing nice to say, I will close these pages for the time being.

A FRANK AND EARNEST LETTER TO TIME

Dear Time,

There are moments when I would like you to slow down and moments when I would like you to fly as fast as you've ever flown before. For your reference, here are some examples:

Slow down

1. When I'm trying to finish writing a story and it's almost time for supper.

2. When I'm reading a really good book and I'm almost to the end and I don't want it to end because I'll never see the characters again. (Why didn't the author write a sequel? You can always write a sequel.)

3. When my bangs won't curl right and I've already used too much hair spray and the bus is clattering up the road, almost to our stop.

Speed up

1. When I'm in the car with The Replacements, who broke up my parents' marriage, and the windows are rolled up tight and it's beyond hot and beyond sticky and beyond uncomfortable and we still have ninety-one miles to go.

Thank you, and fly fast, please.

Sincerely,

Perspiring Profusely Somewhere in Ohio

July 17, 3:11 a.m.

How do you know you're about to break? Is it when your left eye starts twitching and the world wobbles a little? Is it when your back starts cramping up like it's revolting against you and you shift and turn and shift and turn and no position will relieve it? Curled up on the floorboard, legs stretched out across Maggie's lap (that didn't last long, in spite of the shoulder I've given her for the last five hours), pretzeled up against the back window you wish you could shatter for a gulp of fresh air—nothing relieves the cramp.

Is it when you've listened to a three-year-old sing the same song over and over and over again, and you start wishing you were maybe born without the ability to hear?

I can't take it anymore.

Anna finally drifted off again, which eliminated the annoying singing. But there's still the aching body that can't find a tolerable position. And the twitch.

What if it's a permanent twitch? I close my right eye. Can I read with the twitch? I'm relieved to know I can; the words just wobble a little like the world.

Every car that passes illuminates Dad's face in the rearview mirror. His jaw looks tight, his eyes hard and squinty. I wonder how close he is to his own breaking point. I wonder if he's thinking the same thing I am: This was a really bad idea.

Who drives from Texas to Ohio? The stupid, that's who.

At mile one thousand thirty-three (I don't really know the measurements; I'm just guessing and including specificity because it rings truer), Devon squeaked, and I squeezed my eyes shut. Not again.

Devon's crying intensified, making him sound more like a siren, and I knew it would only get worse from there, if the past had anything to teach me. (And it does; that's partly why I keep a journal. Mrs. Barnes said journals are a perfect way to get a little perspective. We think we're going through the Worst Thing Possible today, but tomorrow, when we've survived it, we realize it wasn't as bad as we thought. I don't think Mrs. Barnes has ever been trapped in a car with no air and too many unwelcome people.)

My head split apart and stitched back together in the space of every heartbeat.

Jack shifted on the other side of Maggie. Maggie whispered, "Why does he cry so much?" I shushed her, hoping Lisa didn't hear.

"He's overheated," Lisa said from the front seat. She may have heard. I couldn't be sure.

"Well, we're almost there," Dad said, his voice tight and clipped. "We're not stopping again." Definitive. He's the boss.

At the same time that generous blast of satisfaction collided with my chest, something else did too. I couldn't quite name it. But it made me wonder if this was one of the reasons Mom and Dad didn't work out: Mom was her own boss.

Did they ever fight about that, or did it just burn between them like the oven I once forgot to turn off after taking out the fish sticks and french fries Mom asked me to cook while she rested off a headache?

I knew exactly how much time passed between when Devon started screaming and when we pulled up in Grandma's driveway (one hour, fifty-three minutes). By the time the gravel crackled under the tires, Devon's voice was hoarse and everyone was awake. My head felt like a giant was using it as a kickball in the middle of a rocky field, doing an excellent job of keeping it close to the ground.

It was with pure, blissful relief that I shook Maggie awake

and said, "We're here." She blinked and looked around, like she was confused about where exactly we were, so I added, "Grandma's house." My voice sounded giddy, even to me, but maybe it's just the way three in the morning sounds on me. I've never stayed up this late—or early—before.

We haven't spent nearly as much time with Grandma or at Grandma's house as we have with Memaw. The most we ever saw Grandma was the year we spent in Ohio, when we lived with her for a month or so and then came to visit on weekends and holidays and whenever Mom needed to find out which bar Dad got stuck in.

The house looked the same as I remembered. The garage door sat open, and I could see the black trash bags full of "pop" cans (we call them sodas in Texas, but people look at you a little weird if you say that in Ohio) waiting to be crushed and turned in to the recycling center for a little reward change. The enclosed screen porch, where Dad and Grandpa used to sit smoking cigarettes, watching people pass, was lit by floodlights. Ceramic frogs lined the front walk, the same ones Grandma once caught Jack and me playing with. She yelled at us about destroying property and moving things that shouldn't be moved, even though we didn't do either of those things.

Lisa pulled Anna out and handed her to Dad, then reached for Devon. She shut the Suburban door when she was finished, like she didn't even remember we were here. Maybe she was tired. Maybe it didn't mean anything.

Jack and I looked at each other. Maggie climbed over the seat, since she was the smallest, and opened the door. She had trouble with the release lever, and Dad came over to see what was taking so long.

"You forget how to get out of a car?" His eyes sparkled, but I wasn't entirely sure he was teasing. He pulled a lever that was buried deep under the seat, and the seat slid forward with a whir and a click. Jack and I climbed out and, for the first time in too long, breathed fresh air.

I breathed and breathed and breathed. I didn't know if I'd ever get enough.

I stood under the stars until everyone disappeared into the screened-in porch with its grass-like carpet. (It's as weird as it sounds, yes.)

In the same way I used to wonder if Dad could see the moon I saw through my bedroom window, I wondered now if Mom could see this one, a small white smile in the sky. I tried to smile back, but my lips didn't quite make it.

*G*randma hugged me when I walked through the door. She's tall and has big hands and dyed red-brown hair that looks almost like a glowing orb around her head, at least in the light from the porch. We have a new grandpa. "Charles," Grandma said. He nodded once from his chair but didn't get up to say hello.

Grandpa died of pneumonia three years ago.

"Your mom called," Grandma said. "Wanted to know if you made it all right."

"Jesus, already?" Dad said. "She can't let you kids go anywhere, can she."

He didn't seem to be talking to us, so I didn't answer. I turned to Grandma and said, "Can we call her back?"

"I'll call her back," Dad said, like I was talking to him.

"You kids spend time with the grandparents you haven't seen in three years."

I guess he forgot we lived here for a year, less than three years ago. I also didn't remind him that it was past three in the morning and we hadn't been to bed yet.

Grandma seemed to know, though. "Come on," she said. "I'll show you your room."

I already knew where Maggie and I would be sleeping: The Creepy Doll Room. Grandma has a collection of old porcelain dolls, way too many of them, and she displays them on the bed, on shelves, on tables, beside mirrors, all over the room. Everywhere you look are creepy porcelain dolls. Some of them have eyes that close (and we'll lay these back to make sure they spend the night with their eyes closed instead of staring at us), but most of them don't. Is there anything creepier than turning off the lights, knowing that in the dark there are hundreds of dolls staring at you with smiles on their faces?

Okay, not hundreds. Last time I counted, it was twenty-seven, unless Grandma added to her collection. Which wouldn't surprise me.

At least Maggie would be sleeping with me.

Grandma led us down the hallway to the room at the end. It smelled musty inside, and the dolls were waiting just like they always were. I tried not to meet any of their eyes, tried not to imagine them saying, *Ah, here she is again, the girl who's afraid of the dark. Ready to have some fun?*

They *were* ready to have some fun. I could feel it. I'm hoping I'm so tired their eyes won't make a difference tonight.

I realized, now that I was thinking about it and there were stakes (creepy dolls that might come alive at night) and I didn't want to be in this room, that I didn't know if we were staying at Grandma's or somewhere else for the summer. Would I be able to manage if we were staying right here, in this room, for thirty—no, twenty-nine days? I cut my eyes at the dolls, all of them grinning at me. It was like they didn't even notice Grandma and Maggie.

Grandma was a tower in the room! I willed them to look at her and forget me.

"Where are your bags?" Grandma's voice sliced right through my strange and somewhat morbid thoughts.

"In the car," I said.

I guess I sounded about as weary as I felt, because Grandma said, "Long trip, huh?" Understatement of the decade. She patted my shoulder, and her smile was kind. I don't know Grandma all that well, but I do know she can get inflexible and demanding—Mom called her "extremely particular"—about certain things: the beds being made perfectly, watching *The Price Is Right* without a single interruption every weekday morning, anyone touching her sugar-free candy or her insulin supplies. But I think she's mostly kind.

Missing Mom was a physical ache in both my back and my stomach. I can't remember ever being in Grandma's house without Mom here too.

Maggie and I followed Grandma back out to the living room, where Lisa sat on the couch, Devon in her lap, a bottle sticking out of his mouth. She had one arm around Anna. I was surprised Anna wasn't in bed. I let the brief moment of judgment warm my cheeks.

When Dad came into the room, he said, "I told your mom we're here. It's too late to talk to her, so I told her I'd let you call her on Friday."

Friday's another six days away. But Dad gave us one of those no-arguing looks and collapsed into the chair our new grandpa had been sitting in a few minutes ago. I guess he went to bed as soon as we got here. Dad reclined the chair, propped his feet up, and rested his hands under his head. He didn't look like he had any intention of getting our bags, and I wasn't about to ask him. I figured I was probably tired enough to sleep without washing my face or changing into pajamas or, really, taking off my shoes. Someone might have to wheel me to bed.

A cramp seized my stomach and gave it a good shake.

I thought it must have been something I ate.

I closed my notebook, folded the pen inside it, and carried both of them with me to the bathroom. (The way Dad's been eyeing them reminds me I can't leave them anywhere I'm not.)

As soon as I pulled down my shorts, I almost screamed.

THOUGHTS ON A FIRST MENSTRUAL PERIOD

Oh my God, what is that?!!

I'm dying!

I can't breathe! I CAN'T BREATHE!

This cannot be happening!

Am I dying?

What do I do?!!

No one can ever know!

Oh, please let me die!

Oh my God!

Whyyyyyy?!!

Oh my God, this is awful!

I'm never leaving this bathroom!

I can't go out there and face the world ever again!

Everyone will know! Oh my God, everyone
will know.

Better to just die in this bathroom.

Help!

No! No one come in here! Ever!

Not until the floor swallows me whole!

No no no no no no no!

July 17, 3:52 a.m.

J'm almost certain I don't need to record this entry, because there is no way I will ever forget this moment, but in the case that I actually *am* dying and the cause surrounding my death is mysterious, maybe this note will help determine the cause of death, which appears to be Massive Blood Loss. I don't know the scientific name for that, but it's definitely a scientific reality. All you have to do is take a peek inside this bathroom.

But please don't. At least not until I'm dead.

Blood soaks my underwear, a whole pool of death. Or maybe just Womanhood. It's hard to tell the difference. (Virginia Woolf would like that, I think. Very poetic. And dark. And true.)

Of course there is a perfectly rational explanation for

this pool of death. I learned about it in a video they showed in fifth grade.

But no video can possibly prepare you for this.

No puberty brochure, book about "Your Changing Body," or whispers from other girls ("I got my period this weekend") can possibly prepare you for this.

No mom saying "Take the rest of my Womanhood Supplies, just in case the unexpected Visitor comes to visit while you're visiting your dad" can possibly prepare you for this.

My eyes water, and the whole world goes dark for a minute. I grab the sink in front of me so I don't fall off the toilet and turn this bathroom into a murder scene.

What do I do? My Womanhood Supplies are stuffed at the bottom of my suitcase, which is still out in Dad's Suburban. My underwear is ruined. My jean shorts have the beginnings of a dark stain too.

Don't cry, don't cry, don't cry.

My stomach knots again. Guess it wasn't something I ate.

I stare at the sea turtles lining Grandma's shelves, like they might have the answer to this predicament. They stare back, blank-faced. The seashells don't have an answer, either, I'm sad to report. But when I look at the fish, an answer wriggles into the deepest waters of my brain.

I'll get the bag myself.

I look at the sea turtles again. This time they remind me how far I am from my bathroom at home, decorated with Papaw's old model ships. How far I am from home.

How far I am from Mom.

My vision blurs, but I blink away whatever's in my eyes (it's probably my contacts—I've worn them too long. It's definitely not tears.).

I breathe for a minute before opening the door a crack. "Maggie," I call, so quiet it's almost a whisper. I hope she's still in our room.

Her head pops into view, wearing a shadow, and I almost cry with relief. My plan will need a partner, and there's no way it could be anyone but her.

I guess you get older and grow away from your big brother so you can grow toward your little sister.

Mom would call that a sisterhood. I still call it hard.

RED
(Wound)

You cannot find peace by avoiding life.
—Virginia Woolf

Period (**noun**): a flow of blood (so much more blood than you ever thought possible, so much blood you'll wonder if you're actually dying, so much blood you will never want to see anything the same shade of red or remotely the same consistency again, trust me) and other organic material from the inner parts (specifically the lining of the uterus, but who really knows what *that* is) of a woman (or a girl who is not ready to be a woman; I know what I said about growing up, but not like this), lasting several days (you hope it's only several days and not the rest of your life) and occurring every lunar month (oh, sure, bring the lovely moon into this violent experience) until menopause (or the rest of her life, whichever happens first—and who can be sure she'll survive this first <u>period</u>, considering all that blood loss?).

Some call a <u>period</u> a rite of passage, a girl's

initiation into Womanhood, a necessary step up the ladder of growing up. I say the only passage a period can claim is the kind that makes the world go dark for a short period of time, or what some like to call A Passage Out.

I experience A Passage Out every time I go to the bathroom now. Thanks, period.

J cracked open the bathroom door and listened as Maggie asked Dad if she could have the keys to the Suburban so we could get our bags. I immediately felt bad that I told her to do it.

I heard what Dad said ("I told you I'd get your bags as soon as I rest a minute." It had already been twenty minutes since we got here), but Maggie came back to report anyway, her eyes wide, like she'd just had an up-close encounter with one of the black spiders that live in the holes of our Styrofoam ceiling at home. I wanted to tell her I was sorry, but my Visitor took that moment to make her presence known (again), and I started to panic. Dad wouldn't get the bags, but my Womanhood Supplies were in my bag, and the wad of toilet paper wasn't going to last forever. Maybe not even the next few minutes.

I closed the door on Maggie, along with a quick, "Thanks anyway," and leaned against it for a minute until more of my insides slid out and I remembered why I was shut in this shell-shocked bathroom with turtles and fish and seahorses all staring at me.

Maybe Grandma had something. I knew it was unlikely (she's pretty old), but I rummaged through the cabinets anyway. I found nothing.

I didn't want to ruin these shorts like I'd ruined my underwear, and if Dad's second minute was the same as his first one, I'd have to take matters into my own hands.

I stood up, squared my shoulders, and opened the bathroom door.

Welcome to Womanhood.

I marched into the kitchen, where I'd last seen Dad's keys. If Grandma's garage was still open, I could slip out that way, I thought, and maybe Dad wouldn't even notice. Of course he would notice when I came back in dragging my suitcase, but by then I'd be so close to solving this problem (sort of), I wouldn't care.

Footsteps sounded behind me, but it was just Maggie. "Come on," I whispered. "Let's get our bags."

We went through the kitchen to avoid the living room,

where Dad still reclined, eyes closed. Grandma sat at the kitchen table. The keys were still right where Dad had left them—on the counter beside the rooster cookie jar that never had any cookies because Grandma was diabetic. I always wondered why she kept the jar. I guess some people like cookie jars as decoration.

"You kids hungry?" Grandma said. "I have some left-over meat loaf in the fridge."

She started to stand up, but I said quickly and oh so softly: "No, we just need our bags from the car."

Grandma nodded, and Maggie and I slipped out the door and into the garage, which was still open, hallelujah. Every step squeezed out more of my insides, and I cringed. I wondered if any part of me would be left after all this.

Has a girl ever died of her first encounter with The Visitor? Even if the answer to that question is no, it doesn't mean I won't be the first.

I stuck the key in the back hatch of the Suburban and pulled. Nothing. I pulled again. The hatch didn't budge. I gave it one more try, and it finally popped open with a groan that echoed into the night—or early morning. I winced and said a silent prayer that Dad hadn't heard the noise.

Maggie grabbed her red suitcase and I grabbed my dark-blue one and Jack's forest-green one. I hadn't seen Jack since the minutes after we drove up. I guess he'd shut himself in Grandma's other bedroom. Maybe he was already asleep.

I figured I'd drop the bag at his door.

Maggie and I were almost back into our room when Dad flew out of his chair and into our faces. He smelled like stale cigarette smoke and sweat and something tangy. He pointed a finger at us and said a bunch of words I don't really want to record here, but mostly it was about how he said he was going to get our bags and we're the most impatient kids he's ever known and we're going to learn a thing or two this summer. He looked at me the whole time, and I didn't dare look away.

When he was finished, Maggie and I stood there for a minute, staring at the floor. I sensed Jack behind us, and I imagined him staring at the floor too. My face felt hot with shame and something else, maybe the kind of red-hot anger that slides in slowly and swells and swells and swells until it blasts out in one giant eruption that destroys nearly everything around it.

But I'm not like Dad. I'm not. Besides, I have my journals. I pressed my mouth closed so I could later write the words that were piling up.

Another piece of my insides dripped out, and I remembered why I was standing there with one hand on the bag Dad said I should have left in the car. I could feel the wad of toilet paper withering under the weight of something it was never meant to carry, like I was (that's a little depressing, isn't it—but it's past four a.m. and I haven't had any sleep, so it's probably just exhaustion talking).

"Go on to bed, then," Dad finally said after a minute that felt like a thousand. "Now you have everything you need."

I headed straight for the bathroom, but I didn't close the door before I saw the look Jack lobbed at me from the doorway of his room, like I was already ruining everything. I glared right back.

Come talk to me when *you're* dying, Jack.

I locked the door on him, on Dad, on everything outside this bathroom. I wish I could lock the door on this bathroom, because I do NOT want to do what I have to do. But as Virginia Woolf says, "I will go down with my colors flying."

July 17, 4:19 a.m.

I counted out the Womanhood Supplies: fifteen. How long are periods supposed to last? I hope I'll have enough. I don't even know where to get Womanhood Supplies.

I barely even know how to use them.

I think I put it on right. I hope.

I know I could get all my questions answered—there are two women in this house who have already been through this. But Grandma's old, and there's no way I'm going to talk to Lisa about woman things.

I wish Mom was here. Well, actually, I just wish I was home. I want to crawl into my bed and sleep for however long this unwelcome Visitor lasts.

*M*y stomach cramped just as someone knocked on the door. "Tori, are you gonna stay in there all night?" It was Dad. I could roll my eyes in the bathroom, where he couldn't see me. I didn't remind him that it was no longer night, and, also, it's technically impossible to stay in here all night because I'd already spent all night in the car.

I took a deep breath and smoothed out my voice before I said, "Almost done." Perfectly calm, perfectly steady, perfectly respectful. I even plastered a smile into it. Maybe he could hear it.

"Your little sister needs to pee," Dad said, and at first I thought he was talking about Maggie, but then he said, "It's past her bedtime," and I figured he meant Anna.

What I wanted to say was, *She's not my sister*, but what I said instead was, "I'll be out in a minute."

I guess he couldn't help but have the last word, because he said, "Hurry it up."

I waited until I saw his shadow move away from the gap in the bottom of the door before I wrapped the (really noisy) Womanhood Supply package around the soaked wad of toilet paper and buried it deep in the trash can. I glanced around the bathroom to make sure there were no signs of the crime that happened here, and then I zipped up my suitcase and opened the door.

Dad was nowhere to be found.

Maggie was already sound asleep when I got to our room. I almost turned on a lamp to write this last entry for The First Day of The First Magnificent Summer with Dad (which is technically The Second Day), but I didn't want to see all the dolls. At least in the dark I can pretend they're not here.

Twenty-nine days to go.

A FRANK AND EARNEST LETTER TO MY MENSTRUAL PERIOD

Dear Menstrual Period:

When I said I wanted to show Dad I'm all grown up, that wasn't an invitation.

Sincerely,

Horrified Hundreds of Miles from Home

July 17, around 11:30 a.m.

The oozing woke me up, launched me right up from under the covers and into the bathroom. I moved so fast my feet didn't seem to touch the ground, and, also, I forgot to grab my Womanhood Supplies. So I raced back to the room, checked the hall (for monsters? No. For people. And maybe a few monsters), and raced back into the bathroom, shutting the door softly and turning the lock.

I took a deep breath before inspecting the damage.

It was worse than I thought. How could it be worse than I thought? I have a wild imagination. I imagine all sorts of gory things. But this was worse than I thought. The Womanhood Supply had leaked over the sides and up the back.

Guess I'll need to change this thing more often.

I wish I could talk to Mom. She would know what to do. She would know how many of these I need and where I can buy more (I'm pretty sure the remaining fifteen won't be enough, judging by this morning's alarm—and I mean that in every sense of the word) and what I should do about the ruined underwear. But if I told Mom, she would tell Dad, who would tell Lisa, who would talk to me, and that would just be the worst.

Besides this. This is the worst.

I stripped off another pair of ruined underwear (good thing I grabbed my clothes for the day along with my Womanhood Supplies) and stepped into the shower, hoping no one needed the bathroom for a few minutes. Or the whole day. No telling how long it will take to wash this Womanhood off me.

The water woke up my brain a little more. I remembered The Visitor can last from five to seven days. If it lasted seven, that would mean two of my Womanhood Supplies every day—one in the morning, I guess, and one at night. I tried to think of ways I could make them last longer—wash them out and reuse? No, I think they're meant to absorb, kind of like diapers. But what do I really know?

Nothing. I know nothing.

For a second, despair wrapped around me like a freezing towel. How would I possibly survive this?

But I didn't let it stay for long. I am Victoria Reeves. I can survive anything.

I slipped out of the bathroom and started to head back to The Creepy Doll Room, where I hoped Maggie was still sleeping, so I could climb in beside her and maybe sleep a little more too, but I heard voices in the kitchen. And call it Victoria Reeves's Major Flaw #1 (there are too many to list, really), but I have never been able to hear voices without wanting to hear what they're saying, even if the conversation is not meant for me. I know it's not polite—or even safe, really, if you never want to hear a bad word spoken about yourself—to eavesdrop, but while it's a Major Flaw, it's also a Major Skill. I am practiced at being silent and unseen. I stood behind a doorway when Mom told Memaw she was depressed, when Mom told Aunt Leslie she'd lost thirty pounds and three sizes after the divorce from all the stress and depression, when Memaw asked Mom if she needed any money and Mom said no, she was doing just fine, even though the pantry was almost empty again.

When I was younger, Mom used to catch me all the time. She'd say, "Don't be nosy. This is a conversation for adults."

But practice makes perfect.

As soon as I got close enough to the kitchen, I knew this conversation was for adults too. I almost left, but I heard Dad say, "I don't know, Mom. I'm not sure I can do it. A month is a long time." My mouth dried out like I'd just run to the T and I knew I had the whole way back before Coach Finley would let me stop. (She used to drive behind us in her air-conditioned car yelling, "Come on, girls, no walking." How about some sitting in the back seat of your air-conditioned car, Coach?)

"Wouldn't you be more comfortable staying at the house?" Grandma said. I peered around the corner. Dad had Grandma's shirtsleeve lifted and was rubbing the fleshy part of her shoulder with a cotton ball. He bent over to pick up a vial of something from the table. I only knew it was insulin because I'd seen it before. Grandma doesn't like giving herself insulin shots, and when Dad's around, he does it for her. It wasn't the first time I'd watched him with a kind of horror mixed with fascination.

I didn't even think about how they might look my way and see the shadows of my face or the skin of one hand (I moved it aside) or maybe one creeper eye. I couldn't seem to pull my gaze away from that needle.

Dad jabbed the needle into the medicine container, pulled back the handle, held it up, and flicked it with his finger. "It'll give them something to do," he said. "There's a pool and a lake. We'll have plenty of space."

"They could find something to do at the house too," Grandma said. She winced as Dad eased the needle in her arm (I never knew he could be so gentle), but that was the only reaction she had. I guess after a while you get used to getting shots every day.

"They like camping," Dad said, tossing the now-empty medicine container into the trash and the needle in the sink.

I almost laughed out loud. Dad really thinks we like camping? Does he know us at all? Not if he thinks we like camping. Sure, we used to do it when we were younger, the summers Dad was actually around, but that doesn't mean we liked it. We did a lot of things we didn't like, just to make Dad happy.

The remembering comes in waves, I guess. Like the cramps. I pressed my hands against the place where my butt meets my back, like that would do anything to combat the ache. And of course it didn't. If I don't die from blood loss, I'll die from cramps.

I backed away from the doorway when Grandma said, "I think they'd just like to be wherever their dad is going to be."

Grandma was mostly right, but I added a couple of corrections: We'd like to be wherever our dad is going to be that isn't a campground and that doesn't include The Replacements.

Dad laughed. "Well, I can't take them everywhere with me." I eased one eye around the doorway again and saw him with his back toward me, standing over the sink, probably rinsing the needle so Grandma didn't have to do it later. "They're already driving me crazy. Connie coddles them. They pouted the whole way here." I felt my back stiffen. I smiled the whole way here! I know I did. My cheeks are still sore because of it. Dad stared out the kitchen window and into Grandma's backyard, the one Jack and I once had to rake before going inside to eat a cabbage supper that made me throw up later. Don't ask me why that's the one memory I have of that backyard. The raking and the cabbage might not have even happened on the same day, but that's how my brain has catalogued it. Memory's a wild card. Which is why I try to record everything in my journals as soon as I can after it happens.

I distracted myself with this memory so I didn't have to feel Dad's words sliding into my throat. Already disappointments, in less than a day. That's sure to be a record, but not the kind you want to brag about.

Grandma didn't say anything for a few minutes. Only the rooster clock on the shelf in the kitchen corner made any sound at all, its tick practically deafening. And then she said, "You're a good dad, you know."

And I thought: Maybe that's just something people say.

I watched Dad turn from the sink, wrap his arms gently around Grandma's neck from behind, and drop a kiss on the top of her head. He closed his eyes for a minute, like he was breathing in the smell of her hair. My chest tightened and my contacts must have shifted again, because my vision got all blurry and soft.

"I better go get them up before they sleep all day," Dad said. "Sun only shines for so long."

I raced into the shadows of the hall and slipped back under the covers beside the still-sleeping Maggie, like I hadn't heard or seen anything at all.

*A*fter a brunch of bologna sandwiches and Jones' Potato Chips, Dad told us, "Time to go." We piled back into the Suburban we'd just gotten out of less than twelve hours ago so he could drive us here: a campsite with what looked like a permanently parked RV. (It had potted plants under the canopy. It's been here a while.) The camper looked way too small for all of us, but at least it wasn't a tent.

Dad said, "Get your bags," and climbed out of the Suburban. We had to wait until Lisa got Anna and Devon. She didn't pull the lever on the seat, but we were expecting it this time. At least she didn't "accidentally" shut the door.

I climbed out first.

My bag was a little lighter—I had to change my

Womanhood Supply before we left, which means I'm already ahead of my carefully planned schedule and, in this case, being ahead in any form or fashion is NOT a good thing.

A familiar sound greeted us as we walked toward the RV. Jack's head popped up. He saw her first. "Heidi!" he shouted, and dropped his bag and ran toward her. You wouldn't know he was thirteen by the way he pressed his face into our old dog, the one Dad took without asking. I think he misses Heidi as much as he misses Dad.

Dad waved at a man cooking something at the campsite to our right. It smelled like barbecue chicken. "Thanks for feeding her while we were gone, Gary," Dad said.

The man waved. "No problem at all," he said. He looked at us for a minute, probably waiting for Dad to introduce us, which Dad did not do, and then turned back to his grill.

I wondered how long Dad had been staying here. Was this his home? Was that why Heidi was here? Or had he remembered how much we loved her?

Heidi is a big black-and-brown German shepherd with pink-tinted ears and the kind of bark that makes you stop and listen, like she has something to say.

I followed Jack to where Heidi was chained to a tree. (I tried not to blame Dad for chaining her to a tree; maybe the campground has rules about dogs roaming free.) She licked Jack's face all over. I almost laughed, but Dad followed us over too, and I wasn't sure what he thought about all of it. If I laughed, maybe he would explode in a raging monologue about how he told us to get our bags and we left them in the middle of the campground where they're in the way of . . . nobody?

I snuck a look at Dad. He watched Jack with a half smile, his eyes glassy and crinkled. My chest tightened.

I wanted him to look at *me* like that. How many times has Mom told me it doesn't matter what Dad thinks about me? How many times has Mcmaw said, "What's so wrong with just being you?"

Maybe it does matter what he thinks. Maybe there's a whole lot wrong with just being me. Maybe Mom and Memaw don't know anything.

Maybe I'm hiding behind my humor because I can't stand to—

I think this is The Visitor talking now. How many foreign beings are inside me?

I looked at my hands, curled into fists at my sides. I opened them and took a deep breath. It smelled like dog and freshly mown grass and something sweet, like flowers. Trees lined the sides of the campground, some of them blooming with pretty white flowers.

The smells of barbecue from the campground beside us made my stomach rumble. We had already eaten brunch, but it was more bologna sandwiches. I'm not complaining. I'd just rather eat two slices of airy white bread saturated in mustard than eat more bologna. I'd rather eat one of those white flowers from the trees (they smell sweet and tasty) than eat more bologna. I'd rather eat a pile of brussels sprouts topped with a layer of boiled cabbage than eat more bologna.

Nope. I won't go that far. There *are* some things worse than bologna.

After we said our hellos to Heidi (I didn't let her lick my face, because while I consider myself sort of a dog person, I do not consider myself a dog slobber person), Dad said, "I'll show you where to put your bags." I expected him to head toward the camper, but he moved, instead, toward a small blue tent I hadn't even noticed when we drove up. I watched his back for a minute before following. I was sure my face said it all, so I painted it with another of my plastic smiles.

Lisa, Anna, and Devon had already disappeared into the camper.

Dad unzipped the flap on the tent and said, "Should be plenty of room for your stuff in there, beside your sleeping bags. You'll only be sleeping in the tent, anyway."

Three sleeping bags inside formed a pi symbol.

Why couldn't we sleep in the RV? There must be more

beds than just the ones Dad and his new family would use. We didn't mind sharing. We've gotten good at it over the years, by necessity. Turns out you'll do a lot for necessity.

My throat tightened again. I tried to swallow, but it was getting more and more impossible. I thought I was going to cry. Right there, in front of Dad. But I couldn't. So I shoved it all down, cleared it away, forced my smile in place. "Perfect," I said. My voice sounded like it got shredded in a barbed-wire fence.

Jack stood beside me. He looked at me, and I shrugged, blinked hard. Dad turned around, and I shifted my eyes to the ground, afraid he'd see everything I was thinking in mine. I was never good at pretending, at least not around someone who knows me. I reminded myself Dad didn't know me. Not anymore.

I was safe. Mostly.

But I still locked eyes with the ground like it was the most interesting thing I'd ever seen. Like it was a house made out of books or painted with handwritten stories. Like it was a bowl of chocolate-chip-cookie-dough ice cream that someone was eating in front of me. Like it was Jesse Cox, dribbling a basketball down the court.

(Forget I said that.)

"Well, kids," Dad said, and the tone of his voice turned so serious I looked up. His eyes moved from one of us to another. I held my breath. Was he going to apologize for what he did, the things he said, the way he left us for a brand-new family?

That's not really a Dad thing to do. And his next words confirmed that theory.

"Shit happens."

Okay. I know I just wrote a bad word. And I know I'll probably never forget those words. But in case I do, I want these pages to be a record of my dad's apology for starting a new family before he'd fully left the old one (and by fully leaving, I mean divorced their mother). It was not an apology at all. It was a "suck it up and get over it." Which is, I remember, pretty typical of Dad.

My face burned with a fury I was afraid of. No one said a word.

"It's a nice day," Dad said, looking up at the sky. The sun blazed on a spot near his RV, like it had decided to lend its golden light to the golden Replacements inside. "I'll take you to the pool as soon as we're all settled in." He started to walk toward the camper but then turned around like he'd just remembered something. "There's a bottle in there filled with change," he said. "You can divide it up. Have a little spending money while you're here." He smiled like this should make us smile. I dutifully pinned mine in place. "There's a marina around the corner." He turned around again and called over his shoulder, "Don't spend it all in one place."

The screen door of the RV clicked, and Dad disappeared.

We all stood there looking at each other for a minute before Jack ducked into the tent. I followed him, and Maggie slipped in after me. For who knows how long, we stared at our consolation prize, the giant Ozarka container filled with pennies and nickels and dimes and quarters, until Jack said, "Guess we can dump it all out and divide it up."

At least consolation prizes can be divided up and shared and maybe used to buy something tasty and sweet (I'm talking about you, chocolate-chip-cookie dough ice cream).

July 17, 2:46 p.m.

J don't know how long Dad was collecting change and whether he was collecting it specifically for us in the first place, but by the time we got it all counted out, we each had thirty-one dollars and sixty-seven cents.

We've never had an allowance. Mom doesn't make enough money, even working two jobs—and that's okay. It's not her fault we live, as she says, "paycheck to paycheck" (she uses this term every time Jack says he wishes we could get something at Sonic for supper or Maggie holds up a Lisa Frank folder with her begging eyes or I—no, I am not immune to the temptation of things and stuff—look too long at the latest Mary Downing Hahn book or the newest mannequin display at the mall, on our way to visit the eye doctor).

So having our own money feels like a luxury.

"Want to go to the marina?" Jack said a minute after we finished the division. It was typical. Whenever Jack gets money for Christmas or his birthday, he can't wait to spend it. What Dad said about spending it all in one place? Yeah, Jack will do that.

Me, I like to save money for emergencies.

Like maybe . . . The Visitor catastrophe.

"Where are we gonna put the money?" I said, thinking out loud.

Jack pulled out some ginormous ziplock bags stuffed with clothes. Maggie and I stared at him. My mouth dropped open, and no matter how hard I tried to close it, it wouldn't follow my directions. Jack started shaking out the clothes, which happened to be socks, underwear, and two pairs of wrinkled-up pajamas that looked more like crumpled-up tissue paper than wearable material.

"Why did you bring ziplock bags?" I said. I'm sure Mom was planning to use those bags for something. Everything in our house is perfectly portioned out.

"It keeps things organized when you move your suitcase around," Jack said, dumping out the bag of underwear. My thought at the time: He gets to keep that one. I'll take the one with the pajamas, thanks.

I nonchalantly (one of my favorite words) reached for

the emptied pajama bag. Maggie shot me a dirty look but didn't say anything when Jack handed her the bag that held socks.

"Those were clean, right?" I said, just to be sure.

Jack looked at me like I was stupid, so I guess the answer was yes, although he didn't confirm. Still, I shrugged in Maggie's direction. She started scooping her coins into the bag.

For a minute or two, the only sound inside the tent was coins clanging against each other. The whole inside of the tent smelled metallic and a little bit dirty, like money that's passed through thousands of sweaty palms and . . .

Ew. Sometimes I really don't like you, mind.

I started picking up the coins with my fingertips, one by one, instead of collecting piles in my palms. It took me longer, and I was the last one to finish the task, and Maggie and Jack were staring at me like they couldn't believe I was picking them up like I was, but at least I didn't have the germs of thousands of people's sweaty palms all over my hands. Just on my fingertips.

Jack finally grabbed the last of my coins and shoved them into my bag. I was glad, I have to admit.

"Thank you," I said, and I was completely surprised to note that my throat was thick and my contacts were, again, slipping me The Blur.

Jack gave me a strange look with his dark and bottomless eyes before he settled his gaze on my bag of coins. "What is wrong with you?" he said.

Everything. Everything was wrong with me.

All I said was, "So. Marina?" I elbowed Maggie. "They probably sell ice cream and candy."

"Yes!" Maggie drew out the *s* like a snake hissing.

I almost laughed. Except I was thinking, *Maybe they'll have Womanhood Supplies*, and that killed the mood.

We ducked out of the tent. I glanced toward the RV, which sat silent and still, like no one was even home. Dad said he'd take us to the campground pool (not that I'll be swimming with The Visitor and all). Maybe he'd left without us?

I gave my head a good shake and reminded myself: good thoughts. That's what needs to be in these pages. Good, positive thoughts. Good, good, good. I am not Eeyore. I am not Eeyore. I am not Eeyore.

It's not easy inviting good thoughts when your flimsy tent (it shakes even without a wind) isn't even set up right next to your dad's camper. We're at least half a football field away. It's like Dad didn't want to remind himself we were here.

Maybe he thinks we snore. (And, well, Maggie and Jack do.)

I looked at my watch, a birthday present from Memaw.

It's silver and looks like a bracelet and is one of the prettiest things I've ever owned.

More than half an hour had passed since Dad left us to count out the coins.

"Dad said he'd take us to the pool," Jack said. Stating the obvious.

I shrugged. "Dad's not here," I said, feeling braver because he wasn't. Would I act this unconcerned if he was here? Absolutely not.

"Should we tell Dad where we're going?" Jack said. His eyes narrowed in my direction, like he was challenging me. Wait a minute. Was he trying to say he didn't want to go, he wanted to stay here and wait on Dad and his pool promise? Has he learned nothing in the last two years? Promises don't mean anything.

Again, nothing I would say in front of Dad. Or even Jack. Let him hope. But I wasn't sticking around to see how *that* ended.

I started walking in a completely random direction, I admit. I had no idea where the marina was. But I figured if you followed the road, you couldn't get lost, right?

I hoped that was the case. I hate getting lost. More than that, it could be dangerous. Who knows if there are bears or panthers or snakes. . . .

My hands started to sweat, and I tried to shove the panic back down where it came from, which was somewhere near my stomach. I couldn't tell if it was the earlier bologna sandwich (which I force-fed myself so I didn't have to hear Dad say anything else about picky eaters) that made my stomach feel like it was caught in a blender or if it was hunger. Or, you know, The Visitor.

We hadn't gone more than fourteen steps down the road (I counted them, because sometimes this is an effective way to ignore anxiety) when Dad slammed out of the camper, a towel slung over his shoulder. My heart hammered so hard it hurt my chest. I rubbed it.

Did he hear what I said?

But all he said was, "Running away so soon?" And when no one answered, he said, "You kids ready to go to the pool?"

"We don't have our swimsuits," Jack said. Again with the obvious.

Dad's mouth dropped open, and his green eyes looked like they had lightning sparks in them. "I told your mother to make sure you packed your swimsuits. I swear to God—"

"We don't have them on, he means." I interrupted him because I didn't want to hear what Dad thinks about Mom. Does he know how careful she is to never say a bad word about him? I wish he'd do the same.

But did I tell him? No. Will I? No way. I can pretty much guess how that conversation would go.

"Well, what are you waiting for?" Dad said. "I told you I'd take you to the pool. Did it take you all this time to count out those coins?" He shook his head, like he already knew the answer. But he didn't. He doesn't know anything about us.

My anger tasted like a mouthful of radishes.

We all ducked back into our tent and came back out with our swimsuits. "Where's the bathroom?" Jack said.

Dad rolled his eyes, like either he expected us to change in the tent (uh . . . Jack is a boy and I have The Visitor) or he thought we'd already know where the bathrooms were. He pointed to a brown brick building in the distance, then sat down in a collapsible metal rocking chair to wait. "I'll be right here," Dad said. "But the day isn't getting any younger, and neither am I."

Ha. Ha ha ha.

All the way to the bathroom, I thought about The Visitor and the pool. Can you swim in these Womanhood Supplies? Would swimming wash out all the blood so I could use the supply again? If I got in, would everyone be able to see the blood pooling around me?

All the way back from the bathroom, I thought about how I was going to possibly explain why I was wearing my bikini top but shorts instead of a bikini bottom. (It was much worse than I thought in there. Another underwear casualty. I'd rather not sacrifice my bikini bottoms.)

Maybe Dad wouldn't notice. Like that had ever happened.

Jack and Maggie tossed their clothes back into the tent, but I went all the way inside so I could hide the casualty I carried with me. Dad eyed me like he was about to say something about how long I took or why I was bringing a notebook or what was I doing in shorts instead of a swimsuit, but Jack said, "Can we take Heidi with us?" I could have hugged him for that distraction. Except I think he might have forgotten deodorant again today.

Dad shook his head. "She has to stay on the chain," he said, and he let out a long breath like he was tired. Or maybe sad. Or mad? He's so hard to read. He looked toward Heidi, who watched us with her ears pointed, like she knew we were talking about her. "She got into some chickens near your grandma's house, and I have to keep her with me now."

"What did she do to the chickens?" Maggie said.

Dad shook his head. "You don't really want to know," he said, turning away.

I shuddered.

"Now she stays chained," Dad said. We walked in silence for a minute, staring at our feet (well, I stared at my feet; I'm not really sure what Jack and Maggie were doing, because I couldn't see them), until Dad said, "Don't feel sorry for her. She did it to herself. Maybe this will be a good lesson for her." He lobbed a glaring kind of look over his shoulder. "You can't expect freedom if you go around killing chickens."

Dad, the philosopher. The thought would almost seem the tiniest bit funny, except there were other thoughts shouting for space in my brain.

1. Did we do this to ourselves?
2. And, if so, what is the lesson we're supposed to learn?

J forgot to mention earlier that I brought a friend with me to the pool.

At the bathroom, I took one look in the mirror and did a double take, because I thought I saw a girl with a third eye staring back at me.

Sure enough, right there in the middle of my forehead was a zit big enough to pass as an extra eye. I'm not sure why no one mentioned it. I know Jack doesn't like looking at faces, but this . . . thing . . . is a sight to behold. No wonder Maggie's been looking at me like she's not really looking at me. She's been staring at my friend, talking to my friend, getting to know my friend.

I really hate puberty.

If I'd had a Band-Aid, I would have covered up my third

eye, but since I didn't, I now sit beside the pool, letting it bake in the afternoon sun while I write and it watches Jack and Maggie and Dad swimming and splashing and laughing like they have no third eyes or Visitors or any other cares in all the world.

Maybe I should go dunk my head in the pool. Maybe the excessive chlorine in the water (the smell of it is so strong it stings my eyes, even this far from the pool) would burn off my third eye.

I blame the endless, sweaty trip. My skin might never recover.

For a minute I watched Dad splash around with Jack and Maggie, like the last two years never happened, like he was still our dad, like he never left and found himself a new and better family. My chest ached. I wished I could join them in the water, pretend there wasn't a distance of miles and years between us. Be a real family. Dad sent a wave of water toward Maggie, and she shrieked and ducked and giggled. He swam toward Jack, like a shark, and Jack yelped out of the way.

I remember this dad, when we used to swim at public pools. He was at home in the water. I think he worked as a lifeguard when he was in high school. I always felt safe when Dad came to the pool with us.

It didn't happen often.

My story notebook sits open in my lap, drying. (I'll tell you why in a minute.) A pale-blue umbrella shades me, because I didn't have time to grab the sunscreen. Dad said we don't need sunscreen, we'll tan like he does every summer, no harm done. Mom says we should wear sunscreen all the time, no matter what shade our skin is. She made me promise I'd make sure Jack and Maggie wore it too.

I'm not sure Jack's planning to wear sunscreen this whole summer, after Dad said we didn't need it. He's a different person around Dad.

Maybe we all are. Except Maggie. She doesn't seem to feel the need to be someone different.

And here's why my notebook is drying:

I heard the splash before I saw it. Drops of water hurtled toward me, and I lifted my notebook, but most of them hit their mark.

"Aren't you going to come swim?" Dad said. "Or are you just gonna sit and write the rest of the afternoon?"

I was hoping he wouldn't notice.

I tried to think of something to say, but words felt slippery. I couldn't stop thinking about my notebook pages splashed with water. Had the ink run? Would I be able to read what I'd written? Did Dad ruin even that?

Dad shook his head and narrowed his eyes. "You and that notebook," he said, and the way he said it told me "that notebook" didn't taste very good in his mouth. "You'll write away your whole summer."

He didn't think that was a good thing either.

"I just like to write," I said. My voice sounded thick and wobbly.

Dad's eyes narrowed even more. "What are you writing in there?"

He wasn't really interested. So I didn't really answer. "Things. Stories. Observations." I added: "An opus about growing up."

What could have possibly possessed me to use a word like "opus"? I don't know. Maybe I wanted him to think I'm smart. Maybe I was showing off. Maybe it was a way to prove that I'm all grown up.

Every reason is as sad as another, especially when Dad opened his mouth again.

"You think you're so smart," he said. (It's not a good thing to think you're so smart.) "You think you're too old to swim in a pool?" (It's not a good thing to think you're too old to swim in a pool. My list was growing.) "You think you're too old to play with your family?" (It's not a good thing to think you're too old to play with your family.) He paused, like he was waiting for an answer, but I knew he didn't want an answer. He wanted me to listen. So I did, trying not to let the words too deep inside. Dad pointed to Jack. "Your brother's older than you, and he's out here in the pool, playing." He waited another minute, then sent another wave in my direction, but this time I was ready. The drops didn't hit the notebook, which I held over my head. They hit my face instead. "You think you're so grown-up." Pause, glare, splash. "But you're still just a little girl."

He swam away before I could say anything. Not that I had anything to say, because if I opened my mouth, the only thing I'd do was cry, and that would just make everything worse, including my third eye. (Don't ask me how; I'm just trying to lighten the mood here.) I took a few deep breaths and then focused my attention on my notebook, opening it to the last page I wrote. Too many water drops to count dotted my page, bleeding one word into another. Some of them I could probably fix, but others were lost forever.

Don't cry, don't cry, don't cry.

The lifeguard walked by then, on her way to the chair on the other side of the pool. She paused beside me, her brown ponytailed hair swinging over her shoulder. "Everything okay here?"

I swallowed hard and nodded.

She had dark sunglasses that masked her eyes, but I could tell she was looking at Dad. "He's kind of a jerk," she said, her voice low and soft.

I didn't say anything.

She cleared her throat. "Sorry," she said. "I didn't mean to be nosy."

She looked like she was about to leave, so I said, "That's okay." I guess I wanted to explain things a little, because I said, "We're visiting my dad for the summer."

I could feel her eyes on me, but I didn't look at her. "You know," she said, her voice conspiratorial, like we were plotting something together. "Part of growing up is realizing you don't have to do everything your parents tell you to do. You don't have to be who they expect you to be." She nodded once and added, "I'm Kayla."

I watched her round the corners of the pool and climb into the chair.

I closed my notebook.

For the first time in forever, I couldn't think of anything to say.

A FUNDAMENTAL QUESTION ABOUT THE VISITOR

Why do they call it a *menstrual* period?

Is it because even this—a girl's violent shove into Womanhood—belongs to *men*? A girl gets her first *menstrual* period, and instead of it being "welcome to the world of a woman," it's "welcome to the world of a woman defined by *men*. Dictated by *men*. Made by *men*."

After all, what is a *menstrual* period without *men*?

I've seen the way Dad looks at Jack, like he's some kind of golden child who will walk into a bright and shining future where the world bends to his will just because his last name is Reeves. Sure, he still has words for Jack every once in a while—words come easy for a *menacing menace*—but they're nothing like the *menu* of creatively condemning words he has for Maggie and me, like we're dirty gum stuck to the bottom of a shoe, clutching a hot summer pave*men*t when you just want to walk. We are *men*surable. Jack is limitless.

He carries on the Reeves name? What does that matter? What if I want to keep my last name when or if I ever get married? Can't I be a Reeves too? Can't I carry on the name if I want to? Or is that a crime, Dad?

Or maybe I don't want to carry on a name given to me by a line of *men*. Maybe I'll make up my own last name.

Maybe the *men*tal requirements of those possibilities are too much for Dad's conventional mind. Or maybe Dad's more of a pro at *men*dacity than I thought (yes, I do have a dictionary with me because I love words and I was curious about how many interesting words start with "*men*"—turns out a lot of them are negative words). So good he fools even himself.

But I digress.

And so *men* are even here, in such private places as campground bathrooms with spiders hanging from walls or middle school restrooms where girls go in groups (for moral support and everything) or the bathroom at home with the door that doesn't close all the way. *Men* are where they have no business being, in this brutal and natural and, to be honest, terrifying thing. (I'm still not entirely sure I won't die; I've been bleeding for a whole day now, and there is no sign of stoppage. I just keep trying to think about all the women—not *men!*—who survived their *menarche*—that's a first *men*strual period, by the way—and lived to have . . . how many more?)

Men are everywhere. They have our firsts, our seconds, our praise, our dad's attention.

Can't we at least have this?

Maybe I'll be in the minority here, but I think I'll start calling it womenstruation.

July 17, 6:02 p.m.

he rest of the day passed in a blur: Dad took us to the marina, where Jack and Anna bought some Gobstoppers and Skittles and I'm not really sure what else because I left them to surreptitiously (another great word, don't you think?) look for some Womanhood Supplies. But there was nothing. The shelves were absolutely empty. It's like the people who own this store didn't think a person with The Visitor visiting would ever go camping, and, if they did, they would never need Womanhood Supplies. It's like The Visitor doesn't exist here.

My face burns now, just thinking about it. I won't have enough supplies.

What am I going to do?

At supper Dad brought out a huge silver pot and set it

on the picnic table, on top of two black pot holders. When I peered inside it, my entire body went cold.

It's not that I don't like macaroni and tomato soup with ground-up hamburger meat; it's just that it shouldn't be in this place. This place where The Replacements exist. This place where we are the outsiders. This place where I just want to keep something that was ours—mine and Jack's and Maggie's.

What's so special about macaroni and tomato soup with ground-up hamburger meat (like you don't remember—or maybe you don't)? Every time Dad came home from one of his out-of-state jobs (Was he really working all those months? Who knows?), he would make macaroni and tomato soup with ground-up hamburger meat. It wasn't Mom's favorite dish. She never made it when he was gone, which means it belonged to us and Dad.

Not to them.

But now it was here, and that meant it belonged to everyone.

Dad took one look at my face (why does it have to be such a transparent face?!!) and said, "I'm getting pretty tired of your pouting, Tori."

Words met his, but only in my head. *I'm getting pretty tired of your criticism, Dad.*

If I weren't a coward, I would let them fly.

I tried my best to find something funny to say, but I guess I wasn't feeling all that funny. I'm still not.

I turned my face toward the road so he couldn't see that I was also about to cry. I could feel Maggie's eyes on me, and I launched from my seat and bent over the cooler and lifted out a water bottle, just to have something to do with my hands and my feet and my mouth.

Dad wasn't finished. Is he ever?

"You don't swim with us, you just sit and write in your diary." Dad's mouth twisted, like the word tasted sour to him.

It's not a diary. It's a journal. Maybe that would be more palatable (another great word, I have to say) to Dad.

"You don't buy anything at the store with the money I gave you."

"She bought some candy," Jack said. I didn't know if he was defending me or just stating the facts. You never really know with Jack. I was surprised he'd spoken up at all, though.

Dad's eyes crinkled like he was smiling, but his lips pressed together so hard they lost their color. Then he said, "Oh, thank God she finally participated in something." He shoved a bowl toward me. "I don't want to hear any complaining about what's for supper."

I wasn't going to complain, but he's already made his

assumptions. There's no point in trying to explain anything when Dad's made up his mind about something. I don't know Dad all that well, but I do know it's practically impossible to change his made-up mind. I learned that the first time I listened to him fight with Memaw about something dumb—they fought for an entire hour, maybe longer. Mom used to say they'd both met their match in stubbornness.

What I would give to be sitting at Memaw's table right now.

"We have friends coming for supper," Dad said when he'd scooped bowls for Jack and Maggie. Anna skipped to the table and slid in beside Jack.

"I love macaroni and tomato soup," she announced.

Like she had it all the time. Like she would choose this over any welcome-home meal. Like she couldn't wait to dig in and she'd want seconds and maybe even thirds.

I probably said the same words when I was three.

I tried not to hate her. It's not her fault that we lost everything and she gained everything. But it was hard when Dad smiled at her like that. He said, "You want a lot, Sissy? Or just a little?"

I didn't hear Anna's answer, because someone called out, "Hey, Jerry," and Dad looked up and said, "David, Marsha, just in time." I saw a man with a brown beard flecked with gray, fuzzy hair of the same color, and the kind of blue eyes you notice first in a face, clear and sharp. (I'm trying to work on my descriptive skills, which are really observation skills, for my stories.) The woman had the curliest red hair I've ever seen (it bounced over her shoulders every time she took a step) and so many freckles across her cheeks and nose you'd never be able to count them all. She walked a tiny little dog on a leash, and the dog started yapping when Dad shook the man's hand and clapped his back.

Heidi barked from her chained-up spot, but Jack and I were the only ones who glanced her way. She strained at the chain, and it made my throat hurt.

After saying hello to Dad and exclaiming over how cute Anna looked in a pink ruffled tank top and purple shorts, David and Marsha glanced toward us. Dad extended a hand and said, "My kids from Texas are visiting us for a few weeks." He pointed to each of us. "This is Jack, Tori, and Maggie."

Marsha smiled at us, but before she could say anything, Lisa came out of the RV with another pot.

"I made two," she said, her voice full of something—self-congratulation? Annoyance? Was she looking for thanks that she cooked two pots of Dad's favorite meal, or was she annoyed that it was necessary? Should we eat as much as we can or pretend we're full after the first bowl?

"It smells wonderful," Marsha said.

I agreed. And I wished I didn't.

I thought I might have heartburn, and I hadn't even started eating.

Dad finished dishing out the soup, and for the rest of supper, no one talked to us. Jack and Maggie and I were— are—on the island of misfit toys (no wonder we like that movie so much!), and I'm not convinced there's a thing we can do to escape it.

But that doesn't mean I'll stop trying.

Victoria Reeves never stops trying.

July 17, 8:37 p.m.

*A*fter supper, Dad said, "Tori, Maggie, go wash the dishes so your stepmother doesn't have to do it."

Maggie and I looked at each other. I didn't know if she was thinking the same thing I was thinking, which was, *They're going to let us see the inside of the hallowed camper?* And also, *Why doesn't Jack have to do anything?* And maybe a little bit of, *We didn't come all this way to stand in as a couple of Cinderellas, or, in our case, Cindertori and Cindermaggie.*

But I wiped all those thoughts from my face, wrestled my lips into submission (which probably resulted in a scary smile), and followed Lisa up the shaky stairs and through the door of the RV.

It was so much cooler inside than it was outside. That was the first thing I noticed. If I got to sleep in the camper, I wouldn't be tossing and turning all night, trying to get comfortable in a space that felt completely sealed off from fresh air. Also, I'd have a bed and not the hard ground. (I was assuming here; I haven't actually spent a night in the tent yet. Maybe I'll sleep better than I'm expecting to. Maybe all this smiling and pretending to be happy and compliant and brave and fun and everything Dad wants me to be will exhaust me so much not even Jack's snores will penetrate my deep sleep.)

The second thing I noticed was the smell: cigarette smoke and perfume, like someone sprayed too-sweet flowers all over the place to try to cover up the ashy scent of Dad. I remembered this, too, except Mom preferred citrus scents. You haven't smelled heaven until you've inhaled the scent of mango-orange cigarettes. (I'm being sarcastic. Cigarettes will not be allowed in heaven, because they kill you and they reek, even when mixed with mango-orange. Or the peppermint, spearmint, cinnamon, Juicy Fruit gum Dad pops to mask cigarette-breath.)

The third thing I noticed was that it looked like a home. A brown couch lined one wall, a giant TV lined another, and on the side that looked out on our picnic table was a booth. A small stove and a sink lined the opposite wall.

I imagined them, stuffed together on the couch, sharing a show, maybe snacking on popcorn or Jones' Potato Chips or the giant pretzel rods Dad loves so much. I could see the image, because it was once mine.

My chest throbbed so bad, I thought I'd surely die.

But I didn't.

And we still had to do the dishes.

Lisa showed us where everything went and said, "Just wash and dry them and put them all away. That way they don't take up unnecessary space." Her dark eyes, which seemed an odd contrast to her orangey-red hair, flicked around the camper, like she was trying to remember if she left anything out that she didn't want us to see. Or maybe she was afraid we'd take something.

I tried not to glare when I said, "Okay" as cheerily and eagerly as I could, like doing dishes for the woman who stole my dad was my favorite thing to do in all the world. Maggie shot me a strange look, but I pretended not to notice. I heard Mom's voice in my head: "Are you going to love or are you going to hate, Tori? It's always your choice."

It's just not that simple, Mom.

The Mom in my head talked back: "It's a part of growing up, Tori. We all have to decide who we'll be."

My name is Victoria, Mom.

"It shouldn't take you long to get them done," Lisa said, and I wondered if the words were a sort of warning, like if we took too long maybe Dad would get mad. But I reasoned that if we didn't take long enough, he'd probably also get mad. What was the right amount of time to take?

I almost asked, but before I could, Lisa swung out the door, and it slammed behind her, an exclamation point on our solitary captivity.

I set my notebook down on the counter, far enough away from the sink but close enough so if Dad or someone else came inside, I'd be able to grab it.

No one can read this journal. And I mean no one. Except Future Me. Which is hopefully you.

"I'll dry if you wash," I said, and Maggie nodded.

We're used to doing dishes at home, so it's not like this was a big deal. Mom keeps a dish schedule on the refrigerator, and we take our turns. My dish nights are Wednesdays and Sundays (which are usually fish stick night and spaghetti night, one of them clearly worse than the other as far as dishes are concerned), but that might change once school starts and I have volleyball practice after school.

What made this a big deal was that I couldn't help but wonder what they were doing out there without us, what Dad might be saying about us, what Jack was hearing and doing that we couldn't be part of. Why did he get to stay and we were in here, doing dishes?

I knew why. I remember the look on Mom's face when Dad would tell her (tell her, not ask her) to get him a glass of milk. He'd sit in his brown leather recliner with his feet up and throw the words into the kitchen, where Mom was already fixing breakfast or lunch or supper for us. She'd bring the ginormous glass he kept in the freezer, filled with cold milk, and disappear back into the kitchen, he'd drink it and tell her he was finished, she'd go get the glass and set it in the sink, to be washed and frozen all over again—by her. It was like his legs didn't work when he was home. He didn't lift a hand around the house. He said once that the house was "women's work," and that's the only work they needed to do.

Virginia Woolf once said, "For most of history, Anonymous was a woman." I think Mom wanted to be more than Anonymous, and I think Dad felt threatened by that.

Heavy thoughts for dish duty, I know.

The sounds of Dad and Lisa and Marsha and David and the happy squeals of Anna climbed through the thin walls of the camper. I couldn't hear what they were saying, but I could feel the way it prickled my throat, like I was trying to swallow a ball of sticker burrs. I've never liked being on the outside looking in. If I could justify my eavesdropping habit, that's the closest I'd get to an explanation. A person isn't meant to be alone.

I wondered if Maggie felt the same way. I looked at her from the corner of my eye, but she was in her own world. We worked methodically. Maggie washed and rinsed, handed me the bowl, I swiped it with a towel, piled it up until all the dishes had been washed and dried, and then I put them all away, hoping I remembered the right places. (Even with as little time as he spends in the kitchen, I'm sure Dad would notice if the bowls were where the cups should go.)

It took us half an hour—maybe longer—to finish, and by the time I was done drying, the towel Lisa gave me was sopping wet. I looked around for another, about halfway through, but I couldn't find one, so I dried as best I could. Some of the bowls still had streaks. I thought about using my shirt, but I figured it was probably too dirty. It was quite the predicament, a no-win situation, what Mom likes to call a catch-22: I'm sure I'll get in trouble for leaving the dishes slightly damp, but I'm almost positive I would also get in trouble for poking around in cabinets to find a new towel or using my dirty shirt to dry clean dishes.

I should have made Maggie dry. But no, I don't mean that. Better me than her.

I hung the sopping towel on the stove's handle, the way Mom does at home, then grabbed my notebook.

Maggie and I stepped out the door together, and for a minute I stood there, looking at the scene, Dad with his arm around Lisa, Lisa leaning into him, Anna on his lap, Devon asleep in a small carrier, Jack off to the side, not saying a word, David and Marsha smiling and laughing at something Dad said.

Jack looked up when Maggie and I came out, but I couldn't read his face in the gathering darkness.

"Finally finished?" Dad said.

Yep. Finally finished, Dad.

"About time," Dad said, but his eyes were crinkled and merry, not hard and critical. It was confusing for a minute, until I noticed the beer in his hand. Ah. I remembered this, too. Jolly Dad, two beers in. Sometimes it took three, but always more than one.

Four to six turned him sappy.

More than six turned him mean.

Maggie and I walked to the picnic table, and I opened my notebook.

I tried to lose myself in the story I wanted to tell, but it didn't capture me completely enough to miss what Dad said.

"Tori wants to be a writer."

"That's wonderful," Marsha said.

"Doesn't pay much, unless you're really good at it," Dad said.

Everyone else was quiet. I wanted to say, *Maybe I am good at it.* But I pressed my lips together and pretended I couldn't hear him.

"I'm sure she'll grow out of it," Dad said. "She's still a little girl."

You see the way my pen tried to murder the page there? That's what happens when you have so much to say but you can only say it in secret.

Maybe one day I'll be brave enough to say it out loud.

(I doubt it. Courage isn't my strong point. Is that why people write, because they hide things behind words? I don't know. This is all getting a little too philosophical and I'm still angry and I should probably move to journal #2, where I can write something besides My Depressing Day with Dad. Not such a Magnificent Summer after all.)

July 18, 9:23 p.m.

*Y*es. It has been a whole day since I've written in this journal. An incredibly long twenty-four hours and forty-six minutes.

I know I said I was going to record everything about this trip, and I think promises are made to be kept, but some things just can't be recorded in the moment. They have to be digested first.

Like how much worse the second day of The Visitor is compared to the first day. (You don't even want to know.) Like how I only have five more Womanhood Supplies left now, and I'm pretty sure that's not nearly enough.

Like campground showers.

Last night, after Marsha and David left for the night, Dad told Lisa, "Take them to the campground showers and make sure they wash." Lisa didn't look too happy about this command. I wondered why we couldn't just wait until morning, since we'd been to the pool, but Dad didn't leave any room for negotiation, not even for Lisa. She was tight-lipped when she walked us to the showers, Anna skipping along in front of us.

I'm not sure I can fully describe the awesome horror of these showers. Here are a few of the highlights:

> 1. Spiders everywhere. Clinging to corners,
> way up in the rafters, curled around
> the metal rods holding (astonishingly
> inefficient) shower curtains (I'll come back
> to this), stringing webs between the brick
> walls of the showers. And along with the
> spiders: egg sacks. My favorite.
> 2. The astonishingly inefficient shower
> curtains—you try to pull it all the way to
> the shower wall on one side so no one
> will be able to accidentally see you naked
> (or discover the secret of your Visitor),
> and the other side gapes open. You try to
> carefully attend to the gap in the other
> side, attempting to stretch a nonstretchy
> curtain, and the first side gapes. There

is no closing these shower curtains completely.

3. Which would be okay, if the holding area for dressing and dry clothes actually had a curtain too. Then you'd have double coverage. If one curtain didn't work, you could make the other work. But the dressing area doesn't have a curtain. Which means exposure.

4. How do you dress in a dressing area that doesn't have a curtain? If you're me, you don't.

5. Wet clothes. That's what happens when you bring your towel, your clean clothes, and everything else you may need (Womanhood Supply included) into the shower area along with you. Tonight I tried a better tactic—the Dressing with a Towel Attached Method. I created this method while lying in my sleeping bag last night, listening to the mosquitoes wailing and Jack snoring. I'm happy to report it works!

Here's a step-by-step guide to the Dressing with a Towel Attached Method:

Step 1: Wrap the tiny blue towel your stepmother gave you all the way around you, tucking one top corner into the wrap so it won't fall down.

Step 2: Slip on your underwear.

Step 3: Pull on your pants. It will be challenging, because you're not really dry. Shorts would probably be marginally easier to manage.

Step 4: Put on your bra while still wearing your towel. You might have to estimate where the cups should go, if you're as flat as a piece of bologna.

Step 5: Do not remove the towel yet.

Step 6: Pull on your shirt. When it fully covers your stomach (and only when it fully covers your stomach), go ahead and remove the towel.

Step 7: Adjust things as necessary.

Note: If your Visitor is visiting, things get markedly more difficult.

At least it's good practice for seventh-grade athletics. Still, I have a few questions:

1. How in the world are you supposed to shave your legs in these tiny showers, with spiders hanging over your head like silent timers, no ledge for your feet (and would you want to touch it if there was one?), water spurting out in every direction because the showerheads are awesome, and no dry place unless you want to make friends with those spider-timers?

2. Are you ever truly clean?

Well, at least my hair smells good.

I smelled it all the way through supper tonight, twirling my strands, giving me something to focus on when I felt the familiar lump rising in my throat. As soon as supper was over, Lisa took Anna and Devon inside the camper. Dad followed. All he said was, "Get some sleep, kids." He didn't even look at us when he said it, like we're even less than an afterthought. And the worst part was, I was almost relieved.

I'm not sure I know how to be here or do this without crying.

"Don't be like her," he told me once, when I couldn't swallow the tears. I was young, but those are the kinds of memories that get carved into your brain. *Don't be like her. Don't be like your mother.*

164

Mom. I miss her so much my stomach aches. Just thinking about her made my contacts get all watery again. (I think maybe I rinsed them too much this morning.)

I turned away from Jack and Maggie so they didn't think I was crying. I don't know why I do that. I'm not even the oldest, I'm just the one they think has it all figured out.

Yeah, well, most of the time I don't. Especially now.

Except maybe I do. After a few minutes of thinking, I said, "Want to go call Mom?" My throat still felt thick when I said it.

"Dad said we'll call her on Friday," Jack said. His voice had the tiniest wobble too. The cicadas started singing.

I shrugged. "Dad's not here." I'm only brave when he's not. My voice was quiet when I said the words, but my insides weren't even close to quiet. They roared and twisted. "Come on." I stood up, to have something to do. Settle down that burger Dad grilled tonight.

I didn't wait for Jack and Maggie, I just headed toward the marina, where a pay phone stands just off to the side of the store entrance. I tried not to care if Jack and Maggie were coming with me or not (but I did, if you want to know the truth). I needed to hear Mom's voice.

"Where are you going?" Jack said. When I turned around to face him, he was eyeing the door of Dad's camper. I could hear the television inside, and that made my chest burn so hot I thought Jack would get to tick an item off his bucket list: see someone spontaneously combust. (He's not really morbid; he mostly just likes fire.) The fire moved up into my throat and all the way to my cheeks. They got to watch television in there, and we got to . . . what? Sit out here in nature and pretend we didn't miss home?

I looked up at the sky. The stars winked and sparkled, but not like they did back home. Something stung my leg, and I smacked it nice and hard. The pain spread, then faded.

"I'm going to call Mom," I said. I jingled a few coins I shoved in my pocket before supper. "At the pay phone."

I turned and kept walking.

Footsteps crackled behind me. "Wait up!" Maggie said. Jack caught up just as we reached the first bend in the gravel road. He didn't say anything. The earth and its nighttime creatures spoke loudly enough for us, grasshoppers clicking, frogs croaking and moaning, owls hooting somewhere. No coyotes like back home. But that was okay.

I slid a quarter into the pay phone and dialed Mom's number. I waited for the four rings, then listened to the answering machine. I hung up without leaving a message.

"Maybe she couldn't get to the phone in time," I said. I stuck in another quarter, listened to it click, dialed our number again, four rings, answering machine, hang up.

"What time is it?" I said. My throat felt thick again, my chest tight and hot. Spots dangled in front of my eyes.

"It's eight forty-five here, so seven forty-five there," Jack said.

She should be home from work. She should be answering the phone.

What if what if what if . . .

The scenarios played out in my head in an endless loop. Mom's car flipped on the side of the road. Mom's bones broken in a field, Mom bleeding on the asphalt, Mom collapsed beside a bottle of sleeping pills . . .

No. I tried to steady myself. Deep breath, hold it, let it out. Deep breath, hold it, let it out. One more time.

Maybe it works for other people's minds, but mine still raced with unthinkable possibilities.

I cleared my throat, wiped my sweaty palms on my pants, and put in another quarter, listened to the four rings, answering machine, hang up.

My breath felt tight by this time. A pit opened in my stomach.

What if what if what if . . .

"Tori." Jack's voice came to me from somewhere far away, another planet maybe. He waved a hand across my eyes. "She's not home. We'll call her Friday."

Why is it so easy for him? Why does everything make

sense to him? Why does he not worry that we'll be left alone in the world with a dad who didn't want us?

What if what if what if . . .

"Don't waste all your quarters," Jack said. He put a hand on my arm. My brother, who rarely touches anyone, whose obligatory hugs are awkward and quick like he's desperately trying to get them over with, steadied me with one touch. It was over before I opened my eyes. Jack was looking at me. He nodded toward the marina. "Still open." He jangled some money in his pocket. "Care for some dessert?"

Jack and Maggie moved into the store, a small bell tinkling their arrival or their disappearance, depending on which side of the door you were on.

I stood there for a while, staring at the phone, trying to remember how to breathe.

I want to go home. But sometimes home is the last place you can be, and you have to make do with what you have—a campground with a flimsy tent, spider-infested showers, and a marina that sells chocolate-chip-cookie-dough ice cream. So I squared my shoulders, lifted my chin, and followed my brother and sister into the store, like I was ready to conquer the world—or at least this one.

Of course I tripped over the threshold and the little silver bell practically clanged my arrival.

Well, you know, you can't have everything.

THE FUTILITY OF THE CAMPGROUND SHOWER: A SLIGHT COMPLAINT

Everything about it seemed dirty—the walls, the floor, even the water spitting into my face no matter what direction I moved the nozzle. Bugs crawled everywhere—beetles, June bugs, daddy longlegs—but worst of all were the spiders. I know why they're there; with so many bugs attempting (and failing) a climb up slippery shower walls, The Campground Shower offered a movable feast of the greatest proportion. But there are some places where spiders should not be. I don't want eyes on me in the shower—and I especially don't want eight of them.

How many people have used these showers over the years? The potential answer to that question (hundreds, maybe even thousands) prompted me to shower in my flip-flops. I did not look at the drain, for fear I would see hair that did not belong to me. I did not touch the walls, because other hands (and potentially other body parts) have touched them before.

The steam from everyone's shower (it was uncomfortably crowded tonight) hung in the air, so everywhere felt damp. I would still feel damp, even if I hadn't done my customary Rapid Dry-Off (which Mom says leaves water all over the floor of the bathroom at home, and one day I'm going to kill someone who runs into the bathroom and doesn't see the gigantic water smear—so at least I don't have to worry about that constructive criticism here. The floor's already slippery!). I could spend half an hour trying to dry off, and I would still not dry off.

And where am I supposed to put my soap? I can't very well set it down on the same ledge where everyone else sets down theirs—who knows what sorts of soap pieces (and hair) I might pick up along with my bar. So I held the slippery soap for my entire shower, and even though I lathered and rinsed, lathered and rinsed again, three times total, I can't be certain that when it was all said and done, I was actually clean.

How do you get clean in a place with bugs on walls, spiders in corners, and bits of soap stuck to soap ledges?

There's nothing quite like The Campground Shower.

his morning Dad made pancakes.

It's a complicated thing, these pancakes. They're delicious, like everything else Dad cooks (which isn't much). But they also come with baggage. I wasn't expecting that when I sat down at the picnic table and smelled the perfect combination of butter, milk, flour, and oil (no Aunt Jemima's syrup for me; pancakes aren't supposed to be sweet).

See, way back before Dad left us for another family (or maybe he'd left then, but Mom didn't know it yet and what you don't know can't hurt you), when he came back home after his out-of-state jobs (which, to reiterate, we're not really sure actually existed outside of his imaginary excuses for why he stayed gone so long), he'd usually get in late at night. Mom would let us stay up for a while, watching our favorite movies (*The Goonies* and *The Mighty Ducks* were the best) in the living room, but once it got dark and the clock kept inching past our bedtime (which was eight thirty then), she'd put us to bed with a tight-lipped smile and say, "You'll see him tomorrow morning. The sooner you get to sleep, the sooner you'll wake up and he'll be home." (I wonder now how much of that she said to make herself feel better too.)

The next morning we'd wake up smelling pancakes.

Macaroni and tomato soup for supper, pancakes for breakfast, salt and vinegar cucumbers and Jones' Potato Chips for lunch. And probably a sandwich. But we had sandwiches every day for lunch, so that detail doesn't seem all that important.

Is it strange that I associate Dad's coming home with food?

And now here I was in a campground populated by flies, plasticky smiles (at least on my part), and the smell of Dad coming home. Except that he didn't come home. And he may never come home again. At least not to us.

So today the smell of pancakes made my stomach cramp a little. Or maybe it was just The Visitor. I can't be sure anymore.

The Visitor, in my opinion, is outstaying her welcome. I only have three Womanhood Supplies left.

But I don't want to think about that. I want to think

about pancakes and Dad and jokes that get old for some people but not others.

Dad asked Anna if she wanted a big pancake or a small one. She giggled when she said a big one (because of course he plays the same game with her that he used to play with us). Dad gave her a pancake as big as her plate (and she was not eating off a kid-size plate). When, after eyeing Anna's plate, Maggie said she wanted a small pancake (I guess she didn't remember this game from back when Dad was around), Dad gave her a pancake as small as her fingertip.

And I knew what was coming. He would take us all through the game, because it's supposed to be fun. And it *is* fun. For him. But not for kids who are hungry and just want a normal-size pancake.

Maybe I was a little grumpy. Maybe the plasticky smile was getting stale. Maybe everything about this place—and the people in it—was starting to gnaw on me.

Dad asked me, "Do you want a big pancake or a small one, Tori?"

I said, "Medium size, please." Polite and respectful and everything Dad could ever want in such a short exchange of words.

Dad looked at me twice. I guess he hadn't expected me to answer like I was older than five. When his eyes snagged on mine, I tried not to let him see the words that piled up in my mouth: *Yeah, we grew up, Dad. And you weren't around to see it.*

When Dad turned away, he said, "Well, Tori's no fun. Just a sourpuss pouting."

Why does he always think I'm pouting? Maybe it's just the shape of my lips.

I tried not to let it bother me, but the words needled at my neck. Writing deserves better truth than "Sticks and stones may break my bones, but words can never hurt me," so I'll just go ahead and say it: Words hurt *way* worse than sticks and stones. I sat there, trying to pull out the sticker-burr words. I turned my face away from him and blinked so hard I thought my eyes might never stop shutting and opening. But I didn't want Dad to see what he'd done to me and make fun of that, too.

Dad slapped a tiny pancake onto my plate that couldn't, by any stretch of the imagination, be called medium size. I didn't say anything about it, unless you count "Thank you." I ate it (it only took two bites) and pretended everything was totally fine.

He tried something else with Jack. "How many do you want?" he said. (You have to admire both the persistence and the creativity there.) When Jack said, "Two," Dad slapped down one so big its sides sagged off Jack's plate. Anna giggled. Even Maggie smiled. Jack laughed—a fake, mechanical one, but anyone who doesn't know him wouldn't even notice that. Dad's eyes crinkled up and he said, "Guess Tori's the only one who doesn't find this funny."

And just like that, my brother abandoned me.

I tried not to glare at him, because Dad was looking at me. He said, "You want another pancake, Tori?"

"Yes, please," I said, still perfectly polite and respectful and everything Dad could ever want in such a short exchange of words. I even smiled. Big and wide. Then I added, "A large one, please."

Because sometimes you just have to play the game to survive.

Dad smiled, and in another minute or so, he gave me a pancake that was about the size of two plates.

I tried not to sigh.

"Better eat it all," Dad said. "You asked for it, and we don't waste food here." He couldn't help adding, "Maybe your mama lets you waste food, but not here." And, to underline his point: "Not here."

I used to love Dad's pancakes. But this one tasted like it was sopped in a new kind of syrup called Stale Ash From the Cigarette Dad Smoked Weeks Ago.

You can probably imagine how difficult it was to finish. But I did it. Only to hear Dad say, "Better be careful, Tori.

Those seconds will catch up with you. Too much food has a way of making little girls . . ." He paused. "Hefty."

I don't have to look up what the word "hefty" means. I wish I did.

I also don't have to guess what he thinks of little girls, or maybe my particular brand of little girl (I'm not a little girl, but try telling Dad that—I won't), based on the way his upper lip curled like he smelled something foul—maybe a dead skunk's spray sucked up in the car's air-conditioner vents and blasted into your face during the hottest Texas summer.

After another minute, Dad said, "You want another pancake, Jack? A growing boy should eat till he can't eat anymore."

And I wanted to say, *What about a growing girl?*

But arguing is forbidden, and, like I said, sometimes you just have to play the game.

Even if you don't understand the rules.

*A*fter lunch, where Dad gave Jack two sandwiches and a gigantic bowl of chips, along with a pat on the back and the words "That's my boy. Eat up," and handed Maggie and me one sandwich each and a small bowl of chips to share (I let her have most of them), along with the kind of look that said, "I dare you to ask for more," Dad said, "Get your swimsuits on," and I knew it was going to be bad by the mean gleam in his eyes.

He wiggled his eyebrows and said, "I'm taking you kids to the lake."

You kids. I really hate those words. They sound like we don't even belong to him, like if he had a choice (which he didn't), he wouldn't say, *I'll take those.*

I guess that's why he didn't stay. You don't feel obligated to be a dad to "you kids," only "my kids."

And, as if he was demonstrating my point, he turned to Anna and said, "Go get your swimsuit on, my pretty little Anna."

I really thought I might burn up right there. But spontaneous combustion doesn't happen when you will it. How I wish it did, because the next thing I said was "We're swimming?"

I couldn't believe the words came out of my mouth. Stupid, stupid mouth. I knew we were going to swim; why else would Dad tell us to get our swimsuits on? And the look on Dad's face—that gleeful, challenging, I've-got-a-secret-and-you're-not-going-to-like-it look—told me everything I needed to know.

Just like always, I walked right into his trap.

"There's a water slide your sissy loves," Dad said.

I tried to hide my bristle, but I'm sure Dad noticed, because his eyes narrowed.

She's not my sister, though. She will never be my sister.

Dad didn't say anything. Jack and Maggie and I walked without speaking to the campground showers so we could change. When I rounded the corner into the bathroom, I almost walked into a spider. I screeched. Maggie laughed. It wasn't funny.

Stupid spider.

Stupid campground.

Stupid Replacements.

Why couldn't we just spend the month at Grandma's house or Dad's house or any other house? Why did we have to camp with mosquitoes and flies, which talk to us more (and more nicely) than Dad does? Why do we have to swim in a lake with a water slide and water weeds and all sorts of unknown things living under the surface, just waiting for someone like me (as in: unlucky) to come along?

The events of the morning really made me feel grumpy (or maybe it's still The Visitor making things so difficult), and I needed an attitude change. Walking into a spider on the way out (Yes! Again!) didn't help.

I knew I wouldn't be able to avoid swimming two days in a row—at least not without Dad's wrath, or, worse, his criticism (I've been lashed enough today, I think)—so I put on my whole swimsuit, a giant Womanhood Supply (the old one; I wasn't about to waste a new one) making the back sag. I kept my shorts on because of it.

Now would be a good time to admit what you probably already know, since you're Future Me: I don't like lakes. Not at all. Back when Dad was around more, he used to take us out on Lake Texana. The water was so dark and murky you couldn't even see your hand an inch under the surface. I hated swimming in that lake.

My chest ached all the way back to the campground. But the ache traded places with panic when Dad said, "Now we'll see who's brave enough to go down the slide." He cut his eyes at me, like he knew exactly who *wasn't* brave enough.

It didn't take us nearly long enough to reach the lake, Dad talking the entire way about how great this swimming hole was, eyeing me in the pauses, seeming to say something without saying it.

I heard what he was silently saying.

Are you a coward, Tori?

Can't you see I just want you to have fun?

My God, what a pouty little girl.

I used to hear the words all the time, so they feel familiar and rough and completely and utterly agonizing. This isn't the way it was supposed to be. I guess it was silly to think things would be different now that I've grown up. Maybe I *am* just a silly little girl.

Dad held Anna's hand the whole way to the lake, the same way he used to hold mine. If I had known how to get to the lake, I would have walked in front of them so I didn't have to see her swinging on his arms, wrapping herself around his legs, being lifted and carried when she said her legs were tired.

Has he been around her more than he was around me? Probably. I don't remember ever feeling as comfortable with him as she seems to be.

The sky today is a bright-blue color, no clouds anywhere in it. Weather never really tells the truth of what to expect.

As soon as I saw the murky brown water of my past, I knew it wouldn't be a cloudless, golden-sun kind of day.

I stood there for a while, grasping for a calm place inside, shaking a little, trying not to show it. My throat closed off in that familiar panicky way. My right arm went numb, and I thought maybe I was dying and how that would be a good thing because I wouldn't have to get in the water then, but also I wouldn't be able to see Mom again or any of my friends or Jesse Cox.

I mean, I don't *like* him. I'm just saying. He's a good person to see again.

My breath caught, and I choked. "Something in your throat, Tori?" Dad said.

Only deadly air.

I didn't have to look at him to know he was smiling, and it wasn't the good kind of smile. He didn't even pause before saying, "Go on, kids. Get in the water."

It was an order.

He set Anna down. She splashed right in.

"I need to write something down real quick and then

I'll get in," I said. It was more of a mumble, spoken in such a way that he might not even understand me. Real quick could take hours, maybe. Who was to say?

But Dad turned around. "You're not getting in?"

I glanced at the people stretched out on colorful blankets, dotting the artificial sand. I tried to say something, but Stonehenge was back in my throat, larger than ever.

"I bring you all this way, and you're not even going to get in," Dad said. "My God. Ungrateful—"

I closed my ears.

I *will*, I tried to say. I *will*, I *will*, I *will*. But my throat wouldn't work.

Maybe Maggie thought she was helping when she said, "She doesn't like water she can't see through." I shot her my most sophisticated You're Dead to Me look.

Dad's mouth dropped open. "You mean to tell me your mother spoils you with swimming pools when you live right next to a lake?" His eyes set fire to my face and made breathing much, much harder. "She made a Miss Priss out of you?"

I wanted, in that moment, to open my mouth wide and let loose a string of Mom-defense, to tell Dad that we don't actually go much of anywhere, least of all to pools, because you have to pay to get in, and there's not money for things like that. But I was sure he'd take it personally (and he should, really), and it would just make everything worse. Child support isn't something that comes easy to Dad—not because he doesn't have the money but because . . . well, I don't know. He's already thousands of dollars behind. Mom does the best she can.

Dad doesn't want to hear any of that.

So way before I could swallow the collection of rocks and sludge in my throat, Dad said, "Your little three-year-old sissy isn't afraid to get in lake water, and you are?" He glanced at the slide, gleaming silver in the sun (like a beacon of death) and back at me. "She's not afraid to go down that big slide, and you are?" His eyes were hard and flinty, the green of their rims catching the sun and sending it right straight into the center of my chest, like two laser beams meant to cut out my coward's heart, millimeter by millimeter.

Dad finished with "How ridiculous."

But, no, he wasn't quite finished. As he moved away, he added, "Suit yourself, Miss Priss."

And just like that, I got a new nickname. It wasn't much better than Little Girl.

Dad carried Anna deeper into the water. Jack and Maggie hesitated for a minute, Maggie looking at me, Jack staring at the sand, before moving into the water too, like robots programmed to follow their master.

That's unfair. They're doing the best they can too.

They don't want to be disappointing like me. They don't want to attract the wrong kind of attention from Dad like me. They don't want to see that look leveled at them, the one that says, *And you wonder why I left you.*

I watched them go before opening my journal.

I don't care how much fake sand gets stuck between these pages, what this moment needs is silent words collected on a page. And maybe once I'm done I'll brave the water.

I mean, do I really have a choice?

*M*y minute turned into more than an hour. But I finally got in the water. I did more than get in the water: I braved the slide.

I'm getting ahead of myself, though.

When I finally slipped into the water, trying not to grimace every time my feet hit the mushy mud on the bottom, Dad turned to me and said, "Well, well, well. Miss Priss finally joined us."

Yeah, Dad, I finally joined you.

By this time, The Perfect Child (henceforth, this will be my name for Anna) had already gone down the slide four times.

But rather than say anything (because what was there to say that didn't (a) contain sarcasm—Dad's favorite—or

(b) contain tears of humiliation—Dad's other favorite), I kept moving into the water until it reached my waist.

"I want to go down the slide again," The Perfect Child said. She clung to Dad, since the water was too deep for her to touch bottom.

"Maybe your sissy will take you," Dad said. He looked at me, and I wished, for the billionth time, that he'd stop calling me that.

What else could I do but help The Perfect Child to the slide? She held on to me like an oversize slimy leech. I almost dropped her twice. Who knew wet three-year-olds could be so heavy?

I don't know if I've ever moved so fast through water, cutting through it like something was chasing me (and something probably was, I just didn't let myself stop long enough to think about it). I couldn't stand the feel of The Perfect Child's legs wrapped around my waist and her hands around my neck, so I deposited her as fast as I possibly could onto the slide stairs. (And, okay, maybe I did it a little too roughly, because she stumbled—but I steadied her. I'm not a monster.) I watched her walk all the way up, no hesitation in her step. She'd done this before, and she knew Dad waited at the bottom. He was a safe place for her.

I'd like to say it wasn't fair, but I've learned enough about the world to know fairness isn't the universe's concern.

The Perfect Child flew down the slide and hovered over the surface for a split second before she fell into Dad's arms.

He caught her, of course.

I once went down a slide just like this one, except in a pool. Dad waited at the bottom for me, his arms outstretched. I flew down the slide too, practically weightless then, and hovered over the surface for a split second before crashing into the water and sinking to the bottom.

Dad didn't bother to catch me. He waited a whole three seconds before he pulled me out by a leg.

I watched Dad squeeze The Perfect Child tight and kiss the top of her head, and my contacts slipped and blurred again. I turned away before Dad could see I'd gotten something caught in my eye.

For a second I thought those contacts might be a good excuse to avoid the slide. Dad wears contacts; he knows how fragile they are.

But I knew I wouldn't get off that easily. So I put one hand on the slide's ladder rail.

"Are you really going to slide down?" Jack said in a low voice. I hadn't even noticed him swim up beside me.

Jack knows how much this kind of thing—plummeting into water I haven't been able to fully inspect for creatures and disgusting floating particles and microbes—really terrifies me. But when you don't have a choice, when you have something to prove, when you've been replaced by the kind of little girl who will do whatever her dad says and do it all with a smile and a gigantic dose of courage . . . these are the sorts of things you *have* to do.

I can't be a coward because Dad doesn't like cowards. I can't talk back because Dad doesn't like back talkers. I can't cry because Dad doesn't like crybabies.

I guess what you do when your whole self is disappointing to one of the people you love most in the world is: You change it.

So today I decided to be brave. Today I decided I would not sit on the beach and write, but I would let the dirty water of the lake stain my swimsuit. (I sure hope it doesn't literally stain it; I really like this swimsuit.) Today I decided I would face the slide.

There was hesitation in my step.

I'm sure Dad saw it, the way I stopped at the top of the ladder and looked down at the gleaming silver slide for a whole minute before putting one leg over the top and settling myself on its slick metal. It was cooler than I thought it would be, but it was also much higher than I thought it would be, something you only really notice from the top. It smelled like fish and sweat and dirt.

Hanging so far above the lake didn't bother me nearly as much as thinking about what waited in the water at the bottom of the slide. I was safe so long as I was up there, but I couldn't stay there forever. Some kid behind me yelled, "Are you gonna slide down or what?"

"Or what!" I wanted to shout right back. My cheeks burned. I had to let go of the rail, and I didn't think I would ever be ready.

My heart used my throat as a punching bag while I sat and stared at my toes (the blue nail polish is a little chipped now), the edge of the slide, and the dark-brown water. The lifeguard from the other day—Kayla—watched me from a platform built in the middle of the lake. I swear she nodded.

And eventually I either let go or the kid behind me peeled my fingers from the rail. I closed my eyes for a tiny second before realizing this was a terrible plan if I wanted to know when I was about to hit the water so I could plug my nose and avoid lake water shooting all the way up to my brain, so I wrestled my eyelids open and watched the water race toward me like an ugly brown wall. Fear tasted sour, like the glass of buttermilk Dad once put in front of my breakfast plate so he could watch me swallow and splutter it right back out.

The water from my own body and others' (ew, gross) slid me easily down the slide, which dropped, curved up, and dropped again.

I didn't even scream. I wanted to, but I didn't want to give Dad the satisfaction of hearing my terror.

I felt the slide disappear underneath me, and I hung in the air for a minute, then dropped heavy into the water. I wasn't ready for the way it pulled me under. I sank all the way to the bottom of the lake, where mud and water weeds waited for me. I flung out my arms, trying to slow my progress down, but my efforts came too late. (Panic makes reaction times worse, I've learned.) I felt the slimy weeds wrap around my ankles and pull.

Okay, they didn't exactly pull. But they were there all the same. And they were so slimy I screamed underwater, and then I had a mouthful of lake to either spit out (which is impossible to do underwater) or swallow. Or, option three: hold it in my mouth until I got to the top, which is what I did. (You really think I'd swallow nasty lake water? You know me better than that!)

I almost didn't make it to the top.

Okay, that's also an exaggeration. I had plenty of air left.

Well, not *plenty* of air, but enough. I think. Maybe. Or maybe I could have died in the lake. Maybe Dad would have shaken his head and turned away, another disappointing failure from a disappointing daughter. Maybe Dad would have thought, *Good riddance, then.*

Reading back through that, I'm not really sure what's

gotten into me. I seem to have picked up a parasite that causes extreme negativity, probably from the lake water I held too long in my mouth.

Or maybe it's this place. These people. Dad.

The worst part about that trip down the slide is that when I broke the surface, no one was even watching. Dad was carrying The Perfect Child to the fake beach, his back to me. Jack was climbing up the slide, eyes reaching for the top. Maggie sat on a beach towel, building a castle in the fake sand.

It doesn't matter, though. I know I did it.

I braved the slide, let the lake take me under, but I am still alive.

And that's more than I can say for my Womanhood Supply.

THE STORY OF A SUPPLY

Once upon a time, in a land flowing with crimson milk and honey and other unnameable things, there lived a Womanhood Supply. This Womanhood Supply was just like any other Womanhood Supply: despised (for the most part) but absolutely necessary. And so she lived her existence waiting to be called upon for the most noble of causes—that is, keeping things contained. What things? Certain secret inside things—that's about all you need to know.

This Womanhood Supply was one day chosen as *the* Womanhood Supply, and she fulfilled her duty to the best of her ability, for probably longer than she should have. She kept things, if not neat, then mostly contained. At least, that is, until her possessor wore her into a lake that flowed with certain other unnameable things (just not the same ones mentioned above).

The Womanhood Supply could not swim.

The Womanhood Supply swallowed too much dirty lake water.

The Womanhood Supply swelled up like an overfull, sagging diaper (there really is no other comparison), and that was the end of her life.

Rest in peace, Womanhood Supply. May we never, ever meet again.

July 19, 4:12 p.m.

$\mathcal{T}$he rest of the afternoon I lay on the shore, stretched out on my back, trying to hide the sagging Womanhood Supply that dragged down my shorts in a way I was sure everyone could see. "What's wrong with her butt?" I could imagine them saying. So I smashed it down as well as I could and pretended I was sunbathing. Either the sun burned my face to frying or the humiliation of my sagging shorts did. I'm not really sure which it was.

I do know that my stomach tried, several times, to tie different variations of the knots Jack spent three months obsessed with last year. It kept twisting and folding and clenching up tight.

My Womanhood Supply collection is too quickly diminishing, and the days of Being a Woman apparently don't pass quickly (or dryly) enough.

I tried to distract myself with people-watching, but of course my eyes always snagged on Dad. He periodically waded into the water, holding The Perfect Child's hand, then waded back out to take a sip or a whole chug from his can of beer. I wonder if he drinks because it's enjoyable or if it just takes all those beers to make it through his regular life.

The thought doesn't make me feel any better. Maybe he doesn't even drink when Jack and Maggie and I aren't here.

I think I know better than that (he used to drink all the time at our house), but what do I know of *this* Dad? This Dad, who kisses his daughter. This Dad, who carries her when she says her feet hurt. This Dad, who stays.

I only know what I remember. And I've already established that memory can be a little faulty. (For example, see my first entry of this summer. What a ridiculously hopeful little girl.)

Lisa lay on the sand too, stretched out on her back, same as me, except her towel has dolphins with sparkly eyes on it. Mine's a plain faded yellow towel. Old, with some fringes on one end. Maybe a castoff that was reclaimed for The Replaced.

She's not nearly as pretty as Mom.

There. I said it.

For a while I worked on a story about a girl whose boyfriend left her for another girl who wasn't as pretty as the first, but I gave up after a while, because I don't even have any experience with a boyfriend. I don't know what boyfriends and girlfriends talk about, much less what they do when one leaves the other.

I was so engrossed in my writing, though, that I didn't notice anyone had come near me until water dropped onto the page, smudging words. I looked up, and when I saw Dad, I slammed my story journal shut.

"You and those notebooks," he said, and he didn't look or sound the least bit proud, impressed, or even interested, just mostly annoyed, like I was doing something wrong. Again.

Is it such a crime to write, Dad? To enjoy collecting words on a page, stringing sentences together, telling stories?

He glanced toward the lake. "We're leaving in fifteen minutes. I don't want to hear any whining about not having enough time to swim when all you've done is sit on the sand and write."

Did he spit the words? Almost.

"I think I'll just dry off," I said. I'd been dry for half an hour, BUT my Womanhood Supply was still drenched, and

196

I was afraid (1) it would fall out if I stood up (highly likely, considering the weight of it), (2) Dad would see it (how would you hide a thing like that? Kick sand over it and hope' you covered it in time?), and (3) he would humiliate me by pointing it out to everyone within earshot (it doesn't take too big an imaginative stretch to know that's exactly what he'd do).

I knew Dad expected me to get up and wade back into the water, but I stayed where I was, my notebooks clutched tightly in my hands. I hoped he wouldn't ask to see them. What would I do if he did? Could I tell him they were private journals? Would Dad respect that sort of thing?

He glared at the notebooks for way too long. I thought he might actually take them away, but after a while, his eyes hardened and he turned. I thought I was totally in the clear, but at the last minute he turned back, like he'd remembered something he wanted to say. He nodded toward my notebooks, still gripped in my hands like they could somehow save me (they can, during times like this. But in times when Dad demands to see them or, worse, reads them without asking me—if that happens—they will ruin me).

"What do you write in there?" Dad said.

Maybe he forgot he's asked me this question before. And he doesn't really want to know. He doesn't want to know that he is on nearly every page, that I analyze his new family, that I insert myself into the private places and try to understand why he left us.

He doesn't want to know that I'm not who he thinks I am.

So I said, "Stories and things. A record of my days."

At least I had the good sense not to say, "An opus about growing up" again.

Dad stared at me for a minute, like he was trying to figure out if I was lying. If he had asked to see my notebooks, I would have thrown them into the lake, where the water could soak up every page until the words washed away.

My chest tightens just thinking about it now. All those words, lost. But me, saved.

But Dad didn't ask for them. All he said was, "Seems like a waste of time, writing all day like that," and he moved off toward Lisa and The Perfect Child, who were building something in the fake sand. (Devon was back at the camper with Lisa's mom, who hadn't even bothered to meet us.)

You should have seen the daggers I launched at his back. But words still weaseled in: *Did you leave me because I write so much?*

"Time to go," Dad said, way before fifteen minutes had passed.

I took a deep breath and stood up.

My drowned Womanhood Supply did not fall out.

I thought maybe things were looking up—at least until I tried to walk. I'm surprised no one said anything, like, "What'd you do to your butt, Tori?" or, "Why are you walking like that?" or, "That is the worst wedgie I've ever seen; how can you stand it?"

By the time we reached the campground, my cheeks blazed so hot I thought I might turn to ash.

But, well, here I am.

One more Womanhood Supply down.

July 19, 8:22 p.m.

*A*t supper we ate some fried catfish that was soooooo good and then went for a little walk around the campground. At some point Dad said, "You enjoyed the lake, huh, son?" And Jack said, "It was fun," and the flatness of his tone was lost on Dad. Dad said, "You even went down the slide," and you could tell by the way his voice practically glittered in the air around us that he was proud of Jack.

I went down the slide too, but Dad didn't find my accomplishment necessary to mention. I scowled at the ground, kicking at the rocks on the path.

Dad said, "I sure am glad you came to see me," and wrapped his arm around Jack for a minute before The Perfect Child pulled him away.

I've never felt so invisible in my life. Dad's words made me wonder if he only wanted to see Jack, but Mom insisted that Maggie and I come along too.

But I didn't dwell on it. That's not me (or not the new me, anyway).

When Dad stopped to see something The Perfect Child pointed out, I fell into step with Jack and said, "You okay?" soft enough so Dad wouldn't hear if he caught back up at that exact moment.

Jack didn't look at me when he said, "Yeah. I just *love* swimming in a lake."

I guess Jack wasn't as comfortable with muddy lake water as he seemed to be. I guess maybe he's playing a part too. I don't know him as well as I used to, so I can't even tell.

I almost said something so he would know I understood and that he wasn't alone, but he beat me to words. And he said something extremely surprising. He said, "One of us has to get in the water like Dad expects."

Whoa, whoa, whoa. What was that?

He moved away before I could think of anything to say. Now that I've had time to think about it, I would have said, "Don't you know that you can do no wrong, Jack? You're a boy, carrying on the Reeves name." Or maybe, "Like Dad would have cared if you hadn't gotten in the lake." (I think he was talking about more than the lake, some metaphorical "water," but whatever.) Or even, "You've kind of done this to yourself, you know."

I stopped right there on the path and watched their backs getting smaller and smaller. The sun torched my neck, and my contacts, stupid things, got all blurry again.

Would they notice if I disappeared completely? Probably. And, just my rotten luck, Dad proved my theory correct when he shouted back, "Keep up, Tori. There's nothing to write about while we walk."

If he only knew how very much there is to write about.

Things I Like About Camping

*P*lease read the following choices for "Things I Like about Camping" carefully. Mark the one answer you think is best.

(a) eating outdoors with hungry, stupid, annoying, gross, bountiful, persistent, fearless flies that see no need to back off when food is on its way to a mouth (yes, I accidentally ate one along with a syrup-drenched waffle bite this morning)

(b) swatting away mosquitoes that feed on me while I feed on a burger with cheese and mustard and that's it (absolutely no ketchup, not after . . . well, YOU KNOW)

(c) finding a gnat in the bottom of my glass
when I've already finished my orange juice

(d) absolutely nothing

(a) showering with spiders

(b) walking to an outhouse when I need to use
the bathroom at night (either dragging Maggie
along with me or convincing myself I don't
really have to go. I did both of those last night)

(c) dressing in damp clothes after a pointless
shower so no one sees me naked

(d) absolutely nothing

(a) wading in a murky lake with a muddy bottom
(and that's the good part) and not realizing
the lake has water weeds that will pull at my
feet if I wade too far because my dad thinks
I'm a coward if I don't and who wants to be
called a coward

(b) burning my butt on a metal slide, soaking up
the water runoff from other people's bodies
(how many people do you think pee in this
lake?), sinking all the way down to the slimy
underbelly of the lake

(c) imagining all the snakes and dangerous

creatures headed my way, and I would never even know it because I can't see them in disgusting brown water

(d) absolutely nothing

(a) sleeping in a flimsy tent that flaps even without wind—in fact, it only needs one (or several) of Jack's marvelous snores to whip and shake all night

(b) listening as the buzz of the mosquitoes invading my tent becomes a dull roar, making me wonder if anyone's ever been eaten alive, like literally (I guess zippers don't always keep them out. Also, Dad said Ohio doesn't have bad mosquitoes like Texas, but you probably wouldn't know a thing like that if you're sleeping in a camper)

(c) checking my sleeping bag for poisonous spiders, every night, before I crawl inside it (how do I do it? WITH A HAND! I KNOW! BUT WHAT ELSE CAN I DO?)

(d) absolutely nothing

(a) not knowing what time it is (time is so fluid it's drinkable)

(b) not knowing what we'll do next (will it be
     badminton by the swimming pool with
     holey rackets, sitting at the picnic table
     and cramming another disgusting bologna
     sandwich in my mouth, or twiddling my
     thumbs as the sun starts to sink while I
     wonder how much longer until someone
     comes out with supper?)

(c) not knowing how much longer we'll be
     camping (the important thing is, we'll be
     here awhile, suck it up, get over it, paste that
     smile on your pouty pouty face)

(d) absolutely nothing

(a) counting the beer cans attached to Dad's
     right hand, wondering if there actually *is*
     magic in the world, sprinkled liberally on
     this never-ending supply that seems to come
     from somewhere inside his camper

(b) watching Dad with his campground friends
     and wondering why he has so much to say to
     them and not to us

(c) staring at Dad's backside as he disappears into
     the camper every night with his new family

(d) absolutely nothing

I have no Womanhood Supplies left.

(I thought about calling Mom and begging her to send more, but (1) they wouldn't get here in time and (2) she'd just tell Dad, and who knows what he'd do with this information—make fun of me? Announce it to the whole world? Both and more? No thanks.)

I have no Womanhood Supplies left.

(I thought about sneaking into Dad's camper when Lisa took The Perfect Child and Devon to the marina store today, but (1) I didn't know how long they'd be gone and (2) without a guarantee—like knowing there are actual Womanhood Supplies in there—I just didn't find it worth the risk of getting caught. Dad already has unfavorable opinions of me; I wouldn't want to add "thief" to his long list.)

I have no Womanhood Supplies left.

(I thought about walking the one thousand, two hundred miles home—it's where I'd rather be anyway—but even that wouldn't solve my immediate problem: I have no Womanhood Supplies left.)

How long does The Visitor last?

Too long.

 Black
(Death)

Every secret of a writer's soul, every experience
of [her] life,
every quality of [her] mind is written large in [her] works.

–Virginia Woolf

Period (**noun**): a punctuation mark used to indicate the end of a sentence (a very important one, I might add, otherwise you'd have all sorts of run-on sentences you'd never know when to stop or breathe since <u>periods</u> provide full stops and an opportunity to take a breath and without them you'd keep talking and talking and talking unless you used commas all the time which could get tiresome or you could shout! With exclamation points! Or ask questions? About anything and everything you say? And no one would ever believe you knew what you were talking about? Because if you shout all the time people stop listening! And if all you ever do is ask questions you sound kind of silly? Do you believe yourself? So you see how important the <u>period</u> is I should end this brief aside that's turning into more than a brief aside and conclude the definition this is confusing enough as it is) or an abbreviation

As a writer, I pay close attention to <u>periods</u>, since "varying sentence length is an important consideration in good writing composition," said Mrs Barnes, last year's English teacher I've never known a writer who didn't use <u>periods</u> correctly or just stopped using them at all like I'm doing here although Cormac McCarthy doesn't use quotation marks when people are talking in his books and Virginia Woolf doesn't use apostrophes in contractions in her diaries I find that interesting and a little strange Maybe the <u>period</u> is one of those necessary pieces in life Kind of like a dad

*D*ad said something strange when I sat down to breakfast this morning. He said, "You always in a hurry when you're doing chores?"

I wanted to tell him I'm in a hurry to do everything, especially chores and mundane things like drying off anything with a towel—body included—which is why Mom always complains about water all over the bathroom floor after I shower. There are so many better things to do than drying off with a towel when air works just fine.

Something about his face told me he wouldn't find this at all humorous.

At first I didn't know what in the world he was talking about, but I couldn't ignore the rope of panic that started tightening around my throat. You could tell it strangled me when I said, "What?" at the very real risk of Dad thinking I was a complete idiot.

Dad's eyes narrowed. "Lisa told me the dishes you dried last night and the night before weren't dry at all. Says you just stacked them in the cabinet with water all over them."

Then he looked at me like he really did think I was an idiot. My whole entire mouth went dry, like I'd walked a thousand miles in the desert. And, well, maybe I had.

And then I thought about Lisa, inspecting every dish, reporting to Dad, and I almost rolled my eyes before I remembered I was sitting in front of Dad, not Mom. Mom expects that sort of thing, I think. Dad would probably slap my eyes right out of my head.

So I pressed my lips together, but the anger came splitting out of them anyway. "I dried them!" Did I sound like a whining kid when I said it? I don't think I'm a good judge of that.

But probably.

Still. Lisa only gave me one towel to dry all those dishes, and by the end of the pile, it was already soaked. How do you dry dishes with a soaked towel? I did the best I could.

"Your mother let you get away with that at home?" Dad's smile twisted into what I would call a sneer.

Sure, Dad, go ahead and bring Mom into this. You're

just jealous she's a better parent than you could ever be.

I'm sorry. I shouldn't have written that.

I didn't say anything, just stared at the ground. I could see a tiny ant climbing over blades of grass, and I watched it move with purpose, wishing I could trade places with it. For just a minute. I definitely wouldn't want to spend my life as an ant, where everything, I think, would seem like a predator because you're the smallest thing on earth, besides microbes and phytoplankton and, okay, a lot of things, but still. You're one of the smallest things on earth, and wouldn't you live in fear? I guess that's what I would do if I were an ant.

Is it better to be squashed by a foot or by a dad?

I only have experience with one of those, so I can't say.

"Next time, do better," Dad said, turning to the outdoor grill, where he lined up some breakfast sausages from a Jimmy Dean package. The griddle heated up on the picnic table, plugged into some power near the camper. He was making pancakes again. I wasn't even hungry, but I knew if I didn't eat anything, he'd think I was ungrateful.

"I'm sorry," I said, my breath blowing out with the words. "I'll do better next time."

There was so much more I wanted to say, but I pressed my lips together. I knew he didn't want more than an apology. Dad doesn't like explanations, only submissions.

Maybe I'm weak to give him what he wants, but tell me what you would have done in my position.

Dad didn't seem to hear me, or maybe he didn't think my words were worth acknowledging. He just took a puff of his cigarette and turned the sausages. (Isn't it dangerous to smoke near open fire? I kept waiting for Dad to spurt flames, but after a while, he tossed his cigarette on the ground, perfectly fire-free. I watched the cigarette smoke for a while before it fizzled out completely too. Like it represented my hopes. And what a totally melodramatic thing to say, but you know what? I'm one thousand miles away from home, I'm living in a campground, The Visitor is still visiting, and I have no more Womanhood Supplies. So deal with it.)

After breakfast, Lisa walked out of the camper carrying a basket of clothes, and Dad said, "Tori, Maggie, you'll help your stepmother with the laundry this morning," and at first I resented being ordered around like that, not even asked nicely, until I remembered all my own laundry and the ruined underwear balled up in the zipper front of my suitcase.

At least I'd be able to do my own laundry. Hide the evidence of Womanhood.

"Get your clothes, kids," Lisa said, handing us a trash bag. "We'll wash them at the laundromat in the marina."

All three of us ducked into the tent and stuffed our dirty

clothes in the trash bag. Jack carried it back out, but when he passed Dad and walked like he was going to follow Lisa to the marina too, Dad said, "Your sisters can do it, Jack. We'll go fishing."

Say what?

I know my mouth dropped open for a second, but I managed to lock it down before Dad saw. Jack washes his own clothes at home. He's fully capable of doing his own laundry.

I didn't want to touch those nasty socks! And boys' underwear? Gross, gross, gross, gross, gross!

Jack deposited the trash bag at my feet without even looking at me. Maybe he could feel the anger crackling in the air around me.

There was really nothing I could do if I valued my life. And I do. Very much so.

So we followed Lisa, who carried her own trash bag of clothes, along with Devon in his car seat. (Devon wasn't too important for laundry. But that's probably because he was only a few months old.)

Jack stayed with Dad and *went fishing*. Maggie and I spent half the day washing and drying and folding clothes, me trying hard to hide my underwear from Lisa. I felt her eyes on me every now and then, which made me think I wasn't as good at hiding as I thought.

I have to admit I didn't do a great job folding Jack's clothes. Purposely. Because I shouldn't have to do it.

At some point Lisa gestured to the towels and said, "You can fold those."

Again, more of an order than an ask. I don't like orders.

I also don't know how to fold towels (well, I didn't), because Mom usually takes care of that load at home. So I wasn't entirely surprised to hear Lisa say, "That's not how you fold a towel." She watched me for a second, and I almost missed the rolling of her eyes just before she said, almost softer than I could hear, "Your dad said he had to teach your mom how to fold towels. I thought it was a joke."

My anger swelled fast and furious. It rose in me like a giant wave threatening to obliterate my good sense. I bit down hard on my lip, until I could taste the tang of blood. I swallowed the words, but they rang out in my head like a school bell telling me to get to class.

You are the woman who broke up my parents' marriage, and you dare to say anything remotely unkind about my mother.

Maybe Maggie noticed my agitation. Maybe she could feel the pulsing heat rippling through the fibers of our T-shirts, touching at the sleeves. She said, "Mom does the towels at home."

Lisa's hands stilled, like this bit of news was completely

and utterly shocking. She glanced toward Anna (I decided to start calling her by her name again, no matter what I said before), playing with a bug in the corner (or something . . . I don't really know what she was doing. She was definitely not folding towels) and said, "Even your sister knows how to fold a towel."

And it was too much. Too soon. Too competitive. Too anything and everything. The words would not be swallowed again.

"She's not our sister."

They came out quietly, but they were the loudest thing in the room. For a minute I thought maybe Lisa didn't hear them. But when I finally looked up, her mouth had dropped slightly open, and her eyes had narrowed to slits.

I know she'll tell Dad, and there's nothing I can do about it. I wish I could take them back. I wish I could rewind time. I wish I could have taken a minute to write in my journal so those words could have joined all the others I can never say out loud.

Lisa didn't say anything. She took a towel from the stack, folded it in half, then folded it in thirds. "*That's* how you fold a towel," she said.

The air in the laundromat was stale, so hot it felt suffocating. The smell of the laundry detergent, strong and flowery, totally different from the light lavender scent of the detergent Mom buys, was yet another reminder of how far we were from home.

Maggie and I folded the towels just like Lisa said, careful to align every edge perfectly.

We walked back to the campground together, all of us carrying laundry except for Anna, who skipped ahead. After Maggie and I dropped off our clean laundry at the tent (and Jack's, too. I might have dropped a couple of shirts on the way back from the laundromat, and they may have some dried brown leaves clinging to them, but what's a little dirt?), Lisa said, "Tori" and I knew I was in big trouble. My mouth dried out again, and I turned around, rubbing my chest, which felt like it had invited Jack, his best friend, Brian, and twenty-three other eighth-grade band members to come sit on it and play a little summertime concert, and really, stay as long as they liked.

I didn't look at her.

"Come inside with me for a minute."

Was Dad inside? Was she going to tell on me right in front of my face? Was this my last day alive on this earth?

My legs nearly gave out, climbing up those steps. I breathed long and deep, steeling myself for Dad's fury. But he wasn't inside. Probably still out fishing with Jack. (If I'd been thinking clearly, I probably could have saved myself a little terror. Jack wasn't back yet either.)

I followed Lisa through the door of a bedroom (probably the one she shared with Dad), the bed inside perfectly made with a blue-and-pink flowered bedspread and pink pillows lining the headboard.

Dad sleeps in a pink bed? That made me smile.

Lisa disappeared around a corner. It was a tiny bathroom, with a boxy shower, a toilet, and the smallest sink I've ever seen. Lisa opened one of the cabinets under the sink and pointed inside. I ducked my head, and my face flamed.

An entire collection of Womanhood Supplies lined one side of the cabinet. Lisa said, "I know you got your period. Take anything you need." She handed me a package of supplies, and the relief was so overwhelming I had to blink my eyes to fix my contacts and make sure I could see what was in front of me.

I have enough supplies. I have enough supplies. I have enough supplies.

Now.

"Thank you," I said. It came out like a whisper.

Lisa nodded. I willed her not to say anything else, and maybe it worked. She stood up, her knees cracking. I turned away. Before I was out the door, she said, "All you have to do is ask, honey. For whatever you need."

Her kindness almost made me forget what she'd be

telling Dad later, what she'd already told him about the still-wet dishes. I hesitated for a minute before stepping out of the camper and practically racing to the bathroom up the hill.

I have enough supplies.

Did she mean what she said? People say words all the time. They say words they don't mean, words that twirl away on the wind, words that fade and sizzle into nothing. *I'll see you soon. I'll call you next week. Of course we're not getting divorced.*

I love you.

Words are the easy part, I think.

THINGS I DON'T HAVE TIME FOR (OR INTEREST IN):

Babysitting (how does anybody stand other people's little kids . . . or just little kids in general?)

Making my bed (Mom says it makes a room look tidy and is an easy "win" for the day, but I think it's more of a win for the day when you can drop into bed without pulling down covers. Or feeling trapped by tucked-in sheets)

Playing video games (but I will pretend with the best of them if Jesse Cox likes video games)

Watching soap operas (Dad, on the other hand, loves them. He even records them, so he doesn't miss a single episode if he happens to be out)

Joining a reality television show (*Real World* is the worst. It's not even close to the real world!)

Talking for hours on the phone (just say what you want and need to say and hang up already)

Cheerleading (splits of any kind—air or floor—look so painful they'd probably break me in half)

Excusing boys for being rude or for teasing because it's "just what boys do"

Pretending I'm dumb so I don't intimidate boys with my exceptional brain

Listening to gossip (it doesn't make anybody feel good in the long run, even the person gossiping)

Faking it until I make it

Wearing high heels

Painting my nails (it chips an hour later, unless you paint seventeen coats. Why bother?)

Painting my toenails (yes, I know I have blue polish on my toenails right now, but that's because my best friend, Sarah, made me do it)

Drying off completely after a shower
("completely" is such a subjective word)
Drying dishes
Washing other people's laundry
Folding other people's laundry
Carrying other people's laundry back to their
tent
Doing all that and not hearing a single thank-
you

July 20, 8:54 p.m.

*A*fter supper, before it was even dark, Dad disappeared into the camper, leaving us outside with Anna and Lisa. (Devon was already asleep in the camper.) Anna danced around the fire some before Lisa looked at the door, scooped up Anna, said, "It's time for bed," and carried her inside the camper. Jack and Maggie and I sat there for a while, listening to the sounds of the television we're not invited to watch, as the sun put on a show for us. (It really was beautiful. I wish I'd been able to enjoy it, instead of pretending like I wasn't trying to watch the door of the camper, because Dad didn't even say anything, no good night, no see you in the morning, no welp, that's all I've got for the day. He just disappeared. Who does that?)

I don't know about Jack and Maggie, but first I tried

to figure out what in the world they were watching inside the camper (I don't watch enough television to even give a good guess), then I tried to distract myself by counting the lightning bugs I saw (I made it to seventy-nine before I convinced myself I had better things to do), and finally, when I was about to pull out my notebook and at least pass the time with a story or two, Dad slammed out of the camper with a beer in his hand.

He said, "We're supposed to call your mom tonight," and I thought the sun might have come back up, the world looked so bright.

We got to call Mom.

But there was a problem, and I'll get to that.

We followed Dad to the marina. He picked up the pay phone and used a Post-it note stuck to his pointer finger to dial the number. He didn't even know our phone number? No wonder he didn't call for two years.

I tried to ignore the anger, but it burned my forehead like a fever.

How dare you not know our phone number, I wanted to say.

How dare you make promises you never intended to keep, I wanted to say.

How dare you play with our hearts like that, I wanted to say.

But (1) there is NO WAY I could say any of those things

to Dad, and (2) Mom answered the phone, and everything else sort of just slipped away.

"Connie?" Dad said. My chest throbbed. "I have some homesick kids who want to talk to you." Dad shot a glance at me, and my fever soared, burning my whole face. "They miss you so much they can hardly survive." He didn't wait for her answer before he thrust the phone toward me.

I managed to squeak out, "Mom?"

"Tori!" Mom sounded so relieved to hear my voice that something got stuck in my contacts again. That's what home is, I think: a place where you know you're loved and you don't have to do anything to earn that love.

I sure miss home.

I turned my back on Dad. There was so much I wanted to tell her—I want to come home, Dad wouldn't let us call until today, I hate it here, I hate all of them, he's not at all like I remember (except he kind of is)—but Dad stood right behind me, like he wanted to make sure none of us said anything bad about him or his new family or this place.

Mom said, "You having a good time?" and I said, "Yes," because what else was there to say while Dad's eyes stuck to my back (I could feel them boiling two holes right through me). I couldn't tell her about The Visitor, about the lake slide, about the dishes and humiliation, about how I tried to call her and she didn't pick up and how worried that made me feel—because Dad was *right there*.

"We're swimming a lot," I said.

"That's good," Mom said. She didn't sound distracted, only hollowed out, like the aloneness is harder on her than this visit is on us. And maybe it is. She's never been alone in the house for so long.

I tried to think of something else to say. I could hear the hum of a thousand miles between us. The only mildly safe thing I could think of was, "I'm writing a new story."

"Oh? What's this one about?" I could imagine Mom's back straightening, her eyes glistening. But I couldn't tell her this one is about some kids who race a train across tracks after spending an evening complaining about their parents—and they all die in the end.

She'd call it dark, but dark is all I can seem to write anymore. What happened to my stories full of hope? What if I never find them again after this summer?

"It's a surprise," I said. "Maybe I'll let you read it when I get back home."

Nope. Sorry, Mom. That was a lie.

You see? Words are easy. They spill out of me like they don't recognize the difference between truth and lie. I never let anyone see my work until it's completely finished—and sometimes not even then.

"I look forward to reading it," Mom said. She didn't seem to notice I'd said something untrue.

Dad thumped my shoulder. "Let Jack talk now," he said. My hand clenched the phone so tight I thought I might break it. I didn't want to let Mom go, sever that one connection to home. I know it was childish, but maybe I'm not as grown-up as I thought.

Or maybe every person needs her home more than they ever admit.

"Your dad take you shopping for clothes yet?" Mom said like she didn't hear Dad.

"No," I said. "I think we're going next week." It was a guess, nothing more. Dad hasn't even mentioned shopping for school clothes. Maybe we won't go at all.

That would be a shame. I'm pretty sure it's the only reason Mom let us come all this way. And, honestly, I'd like to have something to show for this horrendous summer besides more bruises on my confidence.

"Give the phone to your brother, Tori," Dad said, louder this time. My chest clenched, sending a cold wave toward my belly. My nose burned—but I *did not cry*. That's the important thing.

At least not where he could see it.

"I have to go, Mom," I said. My voice felt thick and heavy. "But Jack's here."

"Okay. I love you, Tori. And I miss you so much." Mom's voice cracked a little.

"I love you too, Mom." My throat had trouble pushing out the words. I didn't say I missed her, because I'm pretty sure Dad wouldn't like it. I shoved the phone into Jack's hands and tried my best to walk into the bathroom, instead of run, hoping I fooled them all into thinking I just needed to pee.

That's all I need is for Dad to see the hugeness of my homesickness.

But once I locked myself in a stall, the tears streaked down my cheeks. I thought they might never stop, but it turns out Dad's "You finished in there, Tori? My God, you take a long time to poop" is an effective, if temporary, antidote to homesickness.

July 20, 9:03 p.m.

J have one more thing I need to say.

Jack or Maggie must have mentioned that we called Mom once already, or tried, because on the way back to the campsite, Dad said, "I told you we'd call your mother every Friday," and I knew he knew. He didn't say anything else for a minute, like he was waiting for me to say something, deny that I'd been the mastermind behind that disobedient act (in his eyes—but what's an unauthorized call to Mom? A crime?).

I didn't know what he wanted me to say—I'm sorry? I'll never do it again? I missed her too much to wait until Friday? I wouldn't mean the first one, I couldn't promise the second one, and the third one would have been a neon sign pointing to Little Girl instead of All Grown Up. So I said nothing, and the silence thickened and congealed around us until Dad finally said, "I don't like you sneaking around behind my back like that."

Sneaking around? He left us alone while he was in his camper with his new family. We weren't sneaking around, we were trying to find something to do.

But of course I didn't say that. Because maybe I'm a big pusillanimous coward. (I discovered this word—pusillanimous—when trying to explain to my best friend, Sarah, what "pushy" meant and why I thought she was a little pushy when she suggested I ask Jesse Cox to the homecoming dance last year. "Pusillanimous" was the next word in the dictionary. It's derived from two Latin words: pusillus, which means "very small," and animus, which means "mind." People used it a lot in the 1800s, but, tragically, no one really uses it anymore. What a wonderful treasure to lose!)

I tried to stop the words before they forced their way out, but I guess I was still a little shaken by the phone call. I said, "I wasn't sneaking—"

And that was all I got out before Dad swung around so fast, I flinched, the force of his motion blowing away any words I might have said to finish my thought. I squeezed my eyes shut, dropped my head, lifted my shoulders practically to my ears, like my body remembered something I'd long forgotten.

I didn't expect the pain to be words instead of hands. I didn't even have time to adequately protect myself.

"It's pathetic the way you kids lean on your mother and mope about going home. Makes me sick."

The grass on the ground started to blur, and I didn't dare look up. Dad might think it was my eyes, not my contacts.

"Don't sneak around again," Dad said. His blue flip-flops swung around, his hairy toes clutching at them, and I listened to them smack as he walked away.

Back at the campground, I excused myself to the tent, where I watched Dad from the open flap, knowing I was letting in clouds of mosquitoes that would torture us all night. But I can't say I cared (at least not then. Ask me again tomorrow). He smiled and talked with some more campground friends who came over to meet everyone but me. I can't believe how comfortable and easy he is with them.

For a while I kept count of the beers he gripped with white fingers like he was afraid to let them go. (I don't really know if he gripped the beers with white fingers; I couldn't see that far. Have I mentioned my wonky contacts and their constant blurring?)

After the first five, I figured it was probably best not to count.

*W*hy has it been four days since I've written in my journal?

I don't know. I guess I just don't feel much like writing the same things over and over again. How boring it will be for Future Me to pull out this journal and flip to the pages about this summer and read about the humiliation on the giant water slide (not once, but three times!) and the battle to not eat too much. (So far it's easier to count the meals where Dad *hasn't* said something: one.) And the way Dad calls me a little girl like it tastes terrible in his mouth (it tastes terrible to me too). How depressing to be reminded of all the insults Dad wrapped around jokes. ("For a little girl with chicken legs, you sure eat a lot," "How many Toris does it take to dry the dishes?" "What do you call a little girl with pens for hands? A Tori!"). How un-entertaining to walk through such a circular story: Victoria Reeves trying to impress her father, her father never seeming more than annoyed with her, Victoria Reeves rubbing her wonky, blurry contacts, her father ridiculing her for being too emotional (It's the contacts. Really. I still haven't gotten used to them), Victoria Reeves recording volumes of dark stories about kids and their parents, kids who hate their parents, kids who don't have parents, kids whose parents leave them, kids who leave their parents, her father asking her what she writes all day and why and what's so great about stories when there are people she never gets to see standing right in front of her.

At least The Visitor is finally gone.

So if anything changes, you'll be the first to know.

(Also: I did care about the mosquitoes I let in the tent on Friday. They kept me up practically all night, and now I'm pretty sure both Maggie and Jack hate me. Welcome to the club, my friends.)

A PLEA TO A MISSING PART

Dear Sense of Humor,
Where have you gone? Life isn't as much
fun without you.
Sincerely,
Missing My Mirth

July 29, 10:52 a.m.

*J*t's a miracle. Dad is taking us away from this mosquito-fly-all-kinds-of-bug-infested campground, where we sleep on bundles of polyester in a tent with flapping walls, and we're spending the rest of the summer at his house. I don't know what we'll do there, but it's got to be better than this campground, where I don't even have a comfortable place to sit.

After a while the benches start cutting into your legs, and you walk around with stripes on the backs of your thighs, so your dad makes fun of you for "chicken legs that look like they had a fight with some tree bark." Ha ha. So funny, Dad.

He didn't come out and tell us the good news. Of course not. That's not the way Dad works. It happened like this:

There I was, sitting at a picnic table, with my notebook open in front of me. I was working on another story, since there was nothing to write in this journal then. And there he came, slamming out the door of the camper, two dozen eggs in his hands. He looked at me and said, "Waiting for breakfast already?" with that half-amused smile on his face that I completely ignored and, instead, politely disproved with my, "No, I was just writing a little before everyone woke up" (maybe I like to see the sunrise, Dad), and he said, "Better not spend all day writing. Today's the last day here at the campground."

I looked up. His eyes felt like they could burn me right up. "Happy?" they seemed to say. "You got what you wanted."

But I'm not the only one who wants to leave this campground, and he knows it.

Dad looked toward Heidi, who lay with her chin on her paws, staring over at us. He hasn't taken her off her chain the whole time we've been here. Not even for a walk. She walks in half circles and runs a little when Jack plays with her, but that's about all the exercise she gets. I feel sorry for her, chained up like that.

I guess Dad does too, because he said, "Heidi needs a little freedom, and she can't have it here."

He turned around to start cooking the eggs, and I finally

felt safe enough to grin to myself. I opened this journal and started writing the news, and the next thing I knew he ripped it out of my hands and my mouth went dry and my legs went numb and my heart felt like it might crash right through my throat and out into the open, where Dad would see what a blackened, shriveled thing it's become.

I couldn't even tell him to give it back. My tongue felt like a wad of cotton in my mouth.

Dad flipped through the pages, but he did it too fast to read any words. Still, my hands started shaking. If he reads what I've written . . .

The last page is bad enough. I wrote about a memory that came to me the night I lay awake in the tent, swatting away mosquitoes. Dad used to tell me, "Go get Daddy's glass of milk, Sissy," and I would dutifully do it, with a "Yes, Master." It was messed up, and I wrote about it, because, okay, I was mad. Mad about his preference for all things Jack. Frustrated by his constant teasing. Fed up with trying to be who he wants me to be and never quite getting there.

He cannot read this journal.

He didn't. Maybe he saw the look on my face and had a little pity on me. Or maybe he wasn't really interested in my writing in the first place. Maybe he just wanted to torture me for a minute.

Well, it worked.

He tossed the notebook back to me. "I hope you're only writing good things about your family," he said, turning back to the pot he had on the outdoor grill.

I swallowed hard.

If he only knew.

The eggs sizzled when he cracked them. The smell of oil blew toward me, turned my stomach a little. I didn't know if I'd be eating this morning.

But some things you have to force yourself to do, because you know what will happen if you don't. More of the same taunting and teasing, and a person can only take so much of that.

Dad looked over his shoulder. "You're still Daddy's little girl, aren't you, Tori?" The words stuck hard in my chest.

I managed to keep my mouth from dropping open. I also managed to swallow the words that wanted so badly to climb out, which amounted to:

(1) My name is Victoria.
(2) I am not a little girl.
(3) You have another little girl.
(4) You left me, remember?

And then I managed to nod.

Because I'm a coward.

Yes, I'm still your little girl, Daddy. I'll always be your little girl, no matter what you do or say to me or how you treat me like I'm the last one on your love list.

I promise you, I wasn't always so pathetic.

Maggie and Jack joined us at the table, and Dad announced the news to them (not that I was Daddy's Little Girl, but that we were leaving the campground). Maggie asked where his house was, and Dad said it was in the same neighborhood where we'd lived the year we spent in Ohio. Jack and I looked at each other. I don't know if he was thinking what I was thinking, but it sure looked like he might be.

Had Lisa lived right down the road from us all along? Was Dad so close the whole time? Why didn't we ever see him?

"Lisa will go on to the house and get it ready for us. We'll leave tonight."

It will be the first time we've been alone with Dad since we started this summer visit. I tried not to get my hopes up. Hopes don't listen. All I could think was, *We can show him our real selves, let him see what he left behind.*

It's stupid, I know. Why won't my delusions die?

Dad scraped eggs onto Jack's plate first. I couldn't help but notice. Not that I was hungry—but I *was* first at the table.

I told myself it didn't matter. But if I'm writing it, maybe it does. A little.

Lisa left with Anna and Devon right after we finished eating. Dad waved at them from the end of the drive and called out, "We'll be ready around nine or so tonight."

Dad turned around toward us but didn't say anything on his way back into the camper. Jack and Maggie and I looked at each other. I guess things aren't all that different when Lisa's not here.

Maybe he just doesn't know how to talk to us. Maybe he doesn't think we want to hang out with him because we're so quiet when his other family is around. Maybe he wonders if we have anything in common.

Or maybe he just doesn't like us.

We waited a whole hour for Dad to come back out of the camper, thinking maybe he was changing into swim trunks or something, but he never even opened the door. So I said, "Want to go to the marina?" I still had some money to spend. I didn't know if Jack and Maggie did, but I was willing to buy them an ice cream.

"I guess," Jack said, which meant he didn't really want to go, but there was nothing else to do.

"You think we can go swimming without Dad?" I said.

"We should probably ask," Jack said.

"Probably," I said. But Dad's disappearance sure made me want to make him worry.

We all just sat there until I said, "Let me write something down real quick, and then we'll go."

Sometimes I'd like to be the middle child, like I was born to be. Sometimes I'd like someone else to make all the decisions (like Jack, who's older by eleven whole months). Sometimes I'd like to rest.

But in the absence of a leader, I have to be one.

Maybe I'm a little bit angry about that. But what can you do about the life you get?

Live it to the best of your ability, Memaw would say.

I'm certainly trying.

WHAT'S IN A NAME: AN EXAMINATION

Tori

*T*ori Spelling: An actress who plays Donna Martin on *Beverly Hills, 90210*, which is my best friend Sarah's favorite television show. I don't watch it (unless I'm at Sarah's) because (1) Mom thinks I'm not old enough, and (2) if given the choice between a book and a television screen, I'll always pick the book (probably no surprise there—and it's always a choice, because there's only so much time!). From the episodes I've seen over at Sarah's house, I've observed that Donna seems almost obsessively preoccupied with boys. Why? Do we really need them? Typical Tori behavior.

Tori Trees: An American swimmer who competed in

the 1984 Olympics and finished fifth in the women's two-hundred-meter backstroke. Since her win, she's faded into the background of more famous Toris. Typical Tori behavior.

Tori Amos: A singer-songwriter and pianist who broke into the American music scene as a solo artist with the song "Silent All These Years." She was five when she was admitted to the Peabody Conservatory of Music, the youngest student ever. She says what she wants, means what she says, and dares anyone to defy her. She's the kind of person I'd like to be. She is not a Typical Tori, though, because she was born Myra Ellen Amos. Who knows where the Tori came from.

When the letters are arranged backward, Tori spells "I Rot." I most certainly do not. Or at least I don't want to. (This summer is doing a number on me, though.) This is one of the many reasons behind my name change to Victoria. (It was always my name, just not what people called me.)

Victoria

Victoria Beckham: One of five female singers for the Spice Girls, known as Posh Spice. She doesn't take criticism from anybody. She knows who she is, and she's proud to be herself.

Victoria Holt: An English author and my namesake. She wrote Gothic romances and published several books a year in different genres, with different pen names. (Victoria Holt was a pen name; her real name was Eleanor Alice Hibbert.) I've read all her Gothic romances, all her European royalty books (published under the name "Jean Plaidy"), and all her family dramas (published under "Philippa Carr").

Queen Victoria: A remarkable royal who inherited the throne at the age of eighteen and ruled sixty-three years and seven months, longer than any of the kings and queens before her. (She had staying power, because strong women always do, don't they?) A queen—need I say more?

Arranged backward, Victoria spells Airotciv, which, although it's not really a word at all, is arguably better than I Rot.

July 29, 8:49 p.m.

L isa will be here any minute, and I want to get some things down before she comes.

Right before we headed to the marina earlier, Dad walked out of the camper, carrying a bag of giant marshmallows, a mega package of Hershey's chocolate bars, and a box of graham crackers. He had all of it smooshed between his left arm and chest, and in his right hand was—try to guess. It's something to drink, it smells bad, and it comes in a silver can.

Yep. That's right. A beer.

"Where are you kids going?" Dad said. He set everything down on the table, the box of graham crackers thunking to its side, and took a swig of the beer. He clanked it down beside the s'mores supplies (I'm assuming), and a couple of

drops splashed out. I watched them land and almost immediately disintegrate. It was already hot outside.

Yet another thing I won't miss about this campground:
the constant heat. I know I'm from Texas, but I spend most
of my time in The Land of Air-Conditioning.

"We're making s'mores." Dad looked around at us like he
expected more than confused stares. He blinked a couple of
times, then added, "You know what s'mores are, don't you?"

Jack was the one who answered for us: "Yes." Dad narrowed his eyes, until Jack followed up his answer with "We
love them."

Dad seemed satisfied.

It was a little early for s'mores, but we didn't complain.
I'll take graham crackers smothered in goocy chocolate
and marshmallows any time of any day.

I ate three of them before I thought about what Dad
might say later. I put the fourth one back and pretended
I didn't want any more. I watched Maggie and Jack eat all
the s'mores they wanted, and I tried to ignore the longing
in the back of my throat.

After that we sat at the picnic table while Dad talked
about how he used to visit this same campground as a kid
and how he always loved swimming in the lake and the pool
and walking to the marina with a little bit of change his dad
gave him. (His dad wasn't really his dad; his dad left Grandma

before Dad was born, and he was raised by his stepdad. We called his stepdad Grandpa. Dad called him Pop.)

Every time he mentioned Grandma, his eyes got soft.

He disappeared into the camper after finishing his beer, but he always came back out with another. I didn't even care, so long as he came back out.

After four trips in and out of the camper, Dad said, "I don't think your grandma will be around much longer." This time I swear his eyes had tears.

Dad getting emotional? I thought the world might end right there, a spark and a bang and then blackness and whatever comes next.

"Why not?" Maggie said. It was the same question I had, but I was afraid to call attention to myself by asking it. Seeing me might make Dad remember (1) how much he hates seeing me write, (2) how emotional I get, and (3) how many s'mores I'd had. I eyed the box of graham crackers. I *really* wanted another one. Jack had already inhaled the one I'd put back on the paper plate in the center of the table, so I'd have to make another, and that was too risky. I told myself to quit it. Three was more than enough.

Dad took a minute to answer Maggie. When he did, he only said, "She has diabetes. It's taking a toll on her body." He lit a cigarette and pulled in a long breath, lifted his head, and blew out a stream of smoke. I tried not to breathe, since secondhand smoke is one of the most dangerous kinds you can inhale. But I ended up choking, and then I had to try to choke quietly, and have you ever tried to choke quietly? Of course you have; you're me! Sometimes I forget who I'm writing to.

So you know choking quietly is practically impossible.

Dad didn't even look my way.

I kept my eyes on his face. I watched him the whole time he smoked that cigarette, and I swear it wasn't just tears in his eyes, it was sadness all over his face. He looked like a lost little boy. I realized then that he really loves Grandma and that he's afraid of what will happen when she's gone.

I guess we're all complicated people.

Dad sat out there with us the whole rest of the day. Around four he gestured to a cooler near the camper. "Help yourselves to whatever's inside that."

Bologna sandwiches were inside it. I took two apples and two bags of carrots instead. Dad got a bag of Jones' Potato Chips and some sour cream and onion dip, and we dipped and crunched until the first star flickered into the sky.

Dad said, "Go get your stuff. Lisa will be here soon. Jack—take down the tent, and I'll put it in the camper for next time."

Next time—what? He goes camping? We spend a summer with him? He comes to see us?

I rubbed my chest and reminded myself that promises don't mean anything.

We did what he said, and then we sat around the picnic bench again, waiting for Lisa to show up. Dad let Heidi run around the campsite for a few minutes of freedom, and she bounded up to each of us and licked our faces, and I didn't mind it one bit, even though I don't usually enjoy a Face Wash with Dog Slobber.

It was a good day.

I took a last look around the campsite—the thick green trees lined up behind the camper, the flattened grass between our tent and the picnic table that proves we're people of habit and predictability (boring or interesting?), and the gravel path leading to the marina. I didn't even spend all my money.

That's okay. Maybe Mom will let me help with school supplies.

The moon was full and bright by the time Lisa drove up in the Suburban, Anna peering out the side window in the middle row. She grinned when she saw us. I managed to smile back, even if I had to wrestle my lips into submission.

J should know by now that the moon lies.

    The moon lies and the sun lies and the weather lies and the rolling green hills lie and the glittery mud puddles lie and everything lies. None of them tell you what's coming. None of them warn you that the day's about to take a turn you won't like. None of them admit, "I will show you beauty, and then I will make you question whether beauty exists at all."

I should know by now.

I almost didn't write this entry, because I wanted so badly to end on a positive note like "It was a good day." Didn't I know the day wasn't over? But how could it get that much worse?

I'll tell you how: We made it to Dad's house.

That wouldn't seem like such a bad thing, after the campground and mosquitoes swarming in tents and gnats in the bottom of orange juice glasses. But let me tell you a little story you already know. (I just need to write it.)

Once upon a time, there were three kids: two girls and one boy. Once upon a time, their mother sat them down at the table in their Texas kitchen and told them they were moving to Ohio, so they could all be closer to their dad. Once upon a time, they *did* move to Ohio, and they were no closer to their dad except they kind of were and just didn't know it because he never came home.

Dad drove us over bright-green hills you could see even in the moonlight, past homes with neat yards, around Amish horses and carriages (Dad wasn't exactly careful passing them, and I always made sure to wave at them out the back window—an apology of sorts), and after about fifteen minutes of streets I didn't recognize, we turned onto one I did. It was the same street we lived on the year we spent in Ohio.

My mouth went dry. Dad parked in the driveway of a white house with dark-blue trim and the same kind of hill I slid all the way down during Ohio's first snow that year, which lined up perfectly with my birthday and ended with scraped hands, a bruised knee, and, by far the worst to my ten-year-old pride and excitement, three very obvious holes in my brand-new pantyhose.

I felt the air inside the car go tight. I wasn't the only one who recognized the familiar sights.

Jack got out of the car and squinted down the street. We could see our old house from the driveway.

"Home sweet home," Dad said, like he didn't find anything extraordinary about the placement of this house, right down the road—I counted seven houses between this one and the one Mom rented—from the one with rattling noises in the basement that discouraged us from investigating it when Mom left us home alone. (Who knew what sorts of monsters lived down there?)

It was Jack who asked, "How long have you lived here?"

And it was Lisa who answered, "A few years," careless words that meant nothing to her. She answered our question without even knowing it.

Jack looked at me, and I looked at him, and neither of us said a word.

Had Mom known?

Did it make it worse that Dad was so close and rarely made the effort to see his first family? Was he so happy with The Replacements that it didn't matter we were seven houses away, he still wasn't coming home? What did we do that was so bad he couldn't be bothered to be our dad?

I choked when I tried to swallow, and when I felt Dad's eyes on me, I turned away. Maggie took my hand. I don't even think she knew why. Or maybe she did.

Jack led the way inside, because I didn't have it in me. What I really wanted to do was run all the way back to the campground and forget I'd ever seen this house seven houses down from where we lived for a year, where we saw Dad maybe five times in three hundred sixty-five days, give or take a few.

Dad showed us around. Even the house felt familiar, with the circular stairs we loved to race up and down and the same kind of bedroom layout—master bedroom across the hall from the two other bedrooms, a bathroom nearest the stairs. This bathroom had a shower, not a claw-foot tub like ours had.

"You and Maggie will share Anna's room," Dad said, pushing the door open to a frilly pink room with the kind of bed I always wanted as a little girl: a canopied one. I tried not to hate Anna more for having what I always wanted. For taking away my dad.

My chest tightened, and I could feel the panic coming. My vision narrowed and blackened. I leaned against the wall as Dad turned toward the other bedroom.

"And you'll have Devon's room." Jack followed Dad to the other bedroom. "He doesn't sleep in here yet, so you'll have it all to yourself. A boy needs his privacy."

I couldn't even get mad about the obvious unfairness of that. My panic had started to make me sweat. My right arm numbed.

"Are you okay?" Maggie whispered.

I could barely nod. I didn't trust myself to speak. I probably would have wailed instead, so I clamped my lips tight and closed my eyes for a minute, trying to clear my vision.

Panic isn't so easy to explain, but Maggie and Jack are used to it.

"I'll show you the living room and the kitchen," Dad said. "And then it's time for bed."

I managed to make it down the stairs, but it was even worse there. In the living room was our old furniture (Mom had to borrow furniture from Aunt Leslie for our living room at home), in the corner was our old piano (Mom missed that thing so much, but at least Dad didn't sell it like she thought), and in the kitchen was our old table (Memaw bought herself a new table, and I'm pretty sure the only reason she did it was so she could give us her old one). Everywhere I looked was home but not home.

A white blur moved past the back screen door.

"Heidi's out there," Dad said, and opened the door like

he was telling us to go outside. We walked dutifully past him. "There's a pool" (it was a small round kiddie pool with water that came up to my ankles) "and some old bikes you can ride in the morning." Mom's old brown Huffy leaned up against the fence, along with Dad's rusty blue one.

Did he empty out our storage and claim everything as his own? I felt anger bunch up in my stomach like wads of crumpled paper.

I tried hard not to glare at Dad's back when he led us into the house again. I lay awake in my bed for a long time, wondering if I should write this.

And now that I have, I don't feel any better.

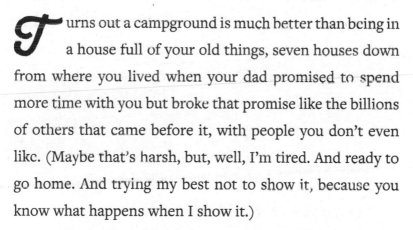

August 6, 4:21 p.m.

urns out a campground is much better than being in a house full of your old things, seven houses down from where you lived when your dad promised to spend more time with you but broke that promise like the billions of others that came before it, with people you don't even like. (Maybe that's harsh, but, well, I'm tired. And ready to go home. And trying my best not to show it, because you know what happens when I show it.)

Did I mention that in this house there is nowhere to go for silence? Dad watches his soap operas at all hours of the day. (He records them and watches them like movie marathons, barking out orders for Lisa—"Get me some ice-cold milk, will you?" "Bring me my pretzel rods." "Just bring me the whole bag of Joneses.") Anna is the chattiest kid I've ever known (granted, I haven't known many, but I think she talks more than I write—which is saying something; how does Dad stand it?) and Lisa's always telling Dad about one thing or another. ("The girls didn't make their beds this morning"—girls, as in Maggie and me; "I found another wet plate in the cabinet," "I don't think Tori's been outside in two days." She thinks she's tattling where I can't hear her, but I hear everything.)

Ten more days until we go home.

I don't even care that we haven't gone school clothes shopping, which Mom asks about every time we call her.

It doesn't help that I have to watch Dad with Anna now. She sits on his lap while he watches his soap operas, leaning her ear into his chest like I used to do. She stands in front of the television, and he tells her he isn't a glassmaker, he can't see through her—just like he used to tell Jack and me. She eats from the bowl of cucumbers soaked in salt and vinegar, the same as I used to.

He even kisses her good night.

Will he stick around for her? Do I want to know the answer to that?

I can't help it. I spend more and more time in my notebooks and less and less time in the Land of People. Dad never smiles at me anymore. He has only hard looks, narrow eyes, and a pinched mouth reserved for my great and unsociable self. I keep smiling as best I can, because Victoria Reeves doesn't give up being who her dad wants her to be, but honestly? My lips are getting sore.

Long into the night I write. I write about how Dad calls me a little girl and I think it's an insult, how it feels like I have to apologize for being a girl, the way Dad compares me to Jack, who he prefers, and Anna, who took my place. I write about Jack joining Dad in the teasing, like he's glad it's not him on the other side of it, and how this builds a thicker wedge between the two of us. I write about Dad's new family, the woman who stole a married man, the answering machine message three years ago that told us everything we needed to know: "Mrs. Reeves, I wanted to let you know your husband's girlfriend is three months pregnant," and the way Mom laughed it off as a prank call.

I write about the agony of being here in this house, the torture of staying under the same roof as the people who destroyed my family, and how much I wish I could blink and be magically back home.

And even though I wrap it all in fiction and poetry, I still put my notebooks under my pillow every night. I don't trust the look in Dad's eyes.

THINGS YOU MISS WHEN YOU'RE MISERABLE

the unbearable Texas summer heat

Mom nagging me to put my stuff away,
    even if I'm about to read the book she's
    pointing to ("You don't need *all* of them."
    Yes. Yes I do.)

fish sticks and macaroni and cheese three
    days a week

Hamburger Helper every other day

a front door you have to practically body
    slam to open

a bathroom door that doesn't quite close
    (probably even when The Visitor visits,
    yes)

folding towels however I want to fold them

dishes my way (which is to say: leaving
   them wet)
rust-colored carpet that clashes with blue
   bedspreads
living in the middle of cornfields with
   absolutely nothing to do on a regular day
   (except read and write)
Texas mosquitoes (which are probably
   more polite and considerate than Ohio
   ones)
the yipping of coyotes that makes it into my
   nightmares
the kind of predictability that seems like
   it could be boring but is really, really
   magnificent
my own bed, which sags in the middle
   because (1) it's old and (2) I sleep in the
   same position every night (unlike here,
   where I spend the nights tossing and
   turning)
tornado scares (invented by my own
   imagination and the slightly stronger
   gusts of wind created by a periodic
   thunderstorm)
missing Dad

August 7, 1:37 p.m.

*W*ith nothing much better to do, I spent the morning writing random poems, lists, journal entries, fiction, nonfiction, whatever I could do to pass the time. Nine days left, and it feels like a lifetime.

Here at the house, Dad likes waking us up by clanging pots and pans and singing a stupid made-up song about lazy kids who sleep the day away. He thinks it's funny, and Jack pretends it is too. I think it's ridiculous, but of course I would never, ever, not in a million years say that. Because Victoria Reeves, as grown-up as she is, won't talk back to her dad.

Is it fear that makes my tongue feel heavy, or is it called Being Female? I don't really know anymore.

Oh, and speaking of Jack, the first day we spent at Dad's house, he walked himself all the way down the street, past the house where we lived for a year, and knocked on a door that had been his best friend's house. Guess what? The friend still lives here. So now Jack's abandoned me and spends most of his time out skateboarding with his old friend Simon.

I knocked on the door of one of my friends' houses, and she no longer lives here. Because that's just my luck. So I spend most of my time pretending I don't exist.

Dad is getting harder to please.

Right after lunch, he said, "You should get outside more, like your brother." I pretended it was just a suggestion, and, also, that he'd left off the part about Jack, who, when we're home, hardly ever goes outside unless he's carrying a fishing pole down to the canal. Five minutes later Dad said, "Don't you have any friends you can visit?" like he wanted to get rid of me, and I said, "They moved away," and he said, "All of them?" and I said, "The ones I remember," even though I'm not sure *all* of them moved away. But I don't remember where the rest of them live. Five minutes after that, Dad said, "Sitting around all day is how people get fat." Yes, he really said this. I ignored it, too, but the words rang out in my head anyway.

Fat fat fat fat fat

Something you don't want to be, that's what he meant.

So I went outside and played with Heidi for a while.

Maggie splashed in the kiddie pool with Anna. (Another betrayal: Maggie plays with Anna all the time here at the house, almost like she's a big sister or something. Doesn't she know she's not supposed to do that?) The sun started burning my arms and neck, so I moved to the shade and opened my notebook again. When I glanced at the kitchen window, Dad was watching, his lips pressed into a thin, straight line. I tried not to read the disappointment in his green eyes, but I've become an expert by now.

At home, Mom doesn't much care about what we do during the summer. I can't wait to get back to that for the last week before school starts. I don't even care if I have nothing to wear. (Dad still hasn't taken us school shopping.) I will make my own clothes just to get away from this suffocating place.

I've finished the entire collection of classics I brought, the volume of Emily Dickinson poetry, and all of Virginia Woolf's diaries. (My favorite quote from them, today, is "I want my marsh, my down, & quiet waking in my airy bedroom." I totally understand, Virginia. You want home. So do I.)

Maybe there aren't enough books to read or words to write to survive The First Magnificent Summer with Dad. Magnificent had a long way to fall, but it sure did fall. Hard.

When I walked back in the house, after maybe an hour

or so outside, Dad pointed to the back door and shook his head. "Get your chicken legs outside," he said. "For at least another hour. You need the sun and the exercise."

What do you think a girl hears when her dad tells her she needs exercise?

You wouldn't be wrong.

August 8, 11:11 a.m.

*T*oday is my best friend's birthday.

I wish I could be there with her.

I wish we could go to the movies, eat at Red Lobster, get ice cream at the mall. (Two scoops of mint chocolate chip sounds absolutely divine.)

I wish I could lie on her bed while she watched *Beverly Hills 90210* and I read another book from her grandma's collection. (She likes Harlequin romances.)

I wish I could go home (no matter how much I sweat walking outside).

I wish I could see Mom.

I wish I enjoyed the outdoors (and sticky humidity and mosquitoes and biting flies and the smoker stench drifting from the back porch—thanks for making it easier to breathe, Dad).

I wish I didn't have chicken legs.

I wish I didn't need exercise.

I wish I didn't bruise so easily. (I'm starting to look a little like Barney—with chicken legs.)

I wish I could make Dad look at me like he looks at Anna. (Sometimes I think he *is* a glassmaker and I'm made of glass and he looks right through me.)

I wish things had turned out differently this summer. (The First Magnificent Summer with Dad has become The First Torturous Summer with Dad.)

I wish The Replacements had never happened.

I wish I didn't need a dad.

I wish I wish I wish.

How many wishes can you make at 11:11?

I make thirteen, to honor Sarah's new age.

And then I beg.

Please please please please please.

Until the clock slides to 11:12.

Time moving forward, instead of back.

I knew wishes were impossible.

August 11, 7:43 p.m.

M om called today. She wasn't home when we tried calling her last night. I have to admit, I felt a little angry about that—so angry I didn't really want to write about it. I still don't want to think about where she might have been on a Friday night.

The truth is, she started dating again right before we left. I know it's only fair—Dad's got a whole new family—but I guess I wasn't ready for it. It feels like Mom dating again writes "The End" to this story I tried to construct in my head, where Dad comes home and we're all a happy family again—like we ever were.

I know it's just a silly little-girl fantasy. I know I'm too old for these kinds of pipe dreams. I know Victoria Reeves doesn't believe in silly little-girl fantasies.

Except she kind of does.

And now I'm talking about myself in the third person. This summer has turned me into someone I hardly recognize.

Anyway, it was still a little early when she called. Dad had just walked through the hall outside our room, banging a pot with a wooden spoon. He thinks we sleep too much. The only one he lets stay in bed is Jack. He says Jack is a growing boy, and growing boys need their sleep. I guess he doesn't think girls grow. Or maybe he just doesn't think they should.

I already had my notebook open when the phone rang. I didn't think anything of it. Grandma calls most days, and I watch Dad's face go soft when he talks to her. Lisa's mom calls too, and her sister. She'll stay on the phone for an hour talking about upcoming garage sales around town.

Dad was putting biscuits in the oven (I never thought I'd say this, but I am all biscuit-ed out. I don't even know how many times we've had Dad's biscuits this summer, but this morning is one time too many. But I'll eat three, at least), so Lisa answered. When she handed me the phone, her face had gone almost as red as her hair. "It's your mother," she said, and she slipped away without another word.

I have to say, I felt a sweet and ugly satisfaction slide into my chest. I wonder what it felt like to talk to the woman whose husband you stole.

The first thing Mom said was "Y'all didn't call me last night. I was so worried."

"We did call," I said. "You didn't answer."

Mom paused for a minute. "Oh," she said. "I guess I thought you'd call earlier."

I almost asked where she was, but Mom offered the details first. "I went out with some friends."

I didn't say anything.

"I've got someone I want you kids to meet."

I started seeing spots.

"He's really nice."

My mouth went dry.

"I think you'll like him."

I couldn't manage to say a single word. Dad kept looking at me, and the shock and horror and maybe a little bit of anger were probably so obvious, they might have been written with an exploding neon marker.

"Tori?"

I finally stammered, "Victoria."

"Right," Mom said. She paused for a minute before saying, "Six more days, sweetie."

Any other day, it would have made me smile that she's counting down, same as me. But today was not a normal day. Today was a day when Mom shattered what little illusion might have been hanging on in my little-girl brain: Dad's not coming back. Ever.

"Has your dad taken you school shopping yet?" Mom said.

"No," I said. I could feel the way the air shifted across the line. It crawled right out of the phone and swung onto my shoulders and pressed down hard. "I'm sure we'll go soon."

Dad was still watching, his mouth and eyes hard. I knew he was going to ask to talk to her.

"He doesn't have much time," Mom said, like she was talking to someone else. Something had changed in her voice too. She was afraid.

People who live with anxiety recognize it in other people. I could feel it all over Mom's words.

What was she afraid of? That Dad wouldn't take us shopping? (We'd figure something out with our old clothes. Maybe I could will my body to stop changing and making things tight in certain noticeable places.) That he would break another promise? (Surprise, surprise, isn't that to be expected?) That he'll keep us for longer than they agreed? (I heard her say this exact thing to Memaw—and if Dad hadn't been standing right there, I would have told Mom she had absolutely nothing to worry about. Dad can't wait to get rid of us.)

Mom said a little more, something about how King, our dog, misses us and mopes around the yard, about how everyone at work has been asking about the visit and how it's going, about the milk she got from the store, like we were home, and how it went bad because she doesn't drink milk. She sounded so lonely, I wished I could wrap my arms around her and never leave the house—and especially not the state—again.

"Let your brother and sister have a turn," Dad said. "It's a long-distance call. You think your mother can afford the minutes you waste saying nothing?"

I felt an overwhelming flash of anger flare in my throat, but I managed to cut off any words that might have crept out.

My voice sounded thick when I said, "I love you, Mom."

"I love you too, Tori. Victoria." She laughed at her mistake. "That'll take some getting used to, I guess." A pause, then: "I'll see you soon."

It sounded like the kind of promise that would carry me through the next six days.

But if I know anything, it's this: Life seems to have a way of twisting up what looks straight and easy.

And, yes, my sense of humor is completely MIA. This is the souvenir I will miserably carry home from The First Magnificent Summer with Dad, along with a stretch of bruised purple skin pulled across my chest, right where the heart is.

(It's not real bruised skin, just so you know—I'm a writer, and writers walk a fine line between literal truth and symbolic truth. It's all the same kind of truth, though. You will not see actual, literal purple skin on my chest, but I'm bruised on the inside. By words, not hands. You remember what that feels like, don't you?)

Metaphorical bruises and literal melancholy. What a way to end the summer.

August 13, 9:22 a.m.

*T*his morning, four days before we're supposed to leave for Texas, Dad announced to the kitchen table: "We're going shopping today."

I was surprised by the massive relief I felt, because (1) I won't have to figure out how to make last year's clothes work, (2) I don't have to add another broken promise to the list of Dad's other ones, (3) Mom doesn't have to worry, and (4) new clothes!

Dad must have seen the relief on my face. His eyes flashed. He said, "What's the matter, Tori?" His mouth pulled up at the corners, but the smile didn't even come close to settling in his eyes. "My little girl didn't think I would take her shopping for school clothes?"

I shouldn't have to repeat this, but I will, because this

is my private journal and I'm entitled to say what I need to say. First of all, I'm not a little girl. Second of all, I'm not *his* little girl; I'm no one's little girl. And third of all, yes, I did think he'd lied about taking us.

I opened my mouth to say something, but then I closed it, fast, afraid the truth would come jetting out, along with the billions of words I've swallowed this summer. I really didn't want to ruin this day or the final four days. I just want to keep the peace and smile and maybe avoid more purple bruises (that no one can see, because they're not real bruises, they're the worst kind: invisible ones) that might not be finished yellowing by the time school starts.

The words piled up inside, stacking against each other.

You told us "See you soon" and you didn't, you told us you'd call tomorrow and you didn't, you told us you'd come home and you never did.

I took a long drink of my milk and tried to wash the words down. I choked, and milk dribbled down my chin. Now I had a milk beard, along with white spots on my favorite blue T-shirt.

Jack watched me with bright, clear eyes, a little wider than normal, but I ignored him. What could I say?

"Where are we going?" I don't know if Maggie asked the question to distract Dad from me and my choking spectacle or if she actually wanted to know the answer. Either way, I shot her a grateful look, which she missed, since she was looking at Dad.

Yeah. She genuinely wanted to know where we were going.

Dad swiveled his head to look at her, and I was glad his attention was off me for a minute, at least. "Nunya," he said, and then he laughed like this was the funniest thing anyone had ever said in the history of talking. ("Nunya" is Dad's nickname for "none of your business.")

"That sounds like a cool place to shop," Jack said, stealing my line. Dad laughed harder and smacked the table with a hand. He thought Jack was fully invested in the joke, but I heard the sharp edges of Jack's voice. I guess he's getting tired of playing a part too.

We packed up and headed to Nunya, the Shopping Superstore for Castoff Kids.

I didn't really care where Dad took us, so long as it was somewhere with clothes I could buy and bring home. At least then Mom would be able to relax a little about the money stuff.

Dad pulled into a massive parking lot that looked like a used-car dealership, it was so crowded.

"Looks like everyone got a head start this morning," Lisa said. She pointed at a parking spot. "Over there?"

But Dad chose to drive around, looking for a closer

space. We ended up driving around for ten whole minutes. While we drove, Dad said, "You'll each have a hundred dollars. Get whatever you want, as long as you can use it for school."

A hundred dollars? After a year of no child support?

I looked at Jack, wondering if he was thinking the same thing: a hundred dollars isn't much when you've outgrown all your clothes and your shoes are falling apart.

It's also not much when you owe at least twenty times that to the mother of your three kids.

"Everything's discounted here," Lisa said as Dad finally swerved into a parking spot, the tires screeching like he'd reached his last thread of patience. At first I thought she could maybe read my mind, but then she said, "So before we buy anything, we'll have to check it for flaws."

It's a clothing warehouse where stores send their leftovers. I tried not to think about how this perfectly described us.

Some kids you check for flaws and they're too defective to take back home.

Happy shopping!

August 13, 3:33 p.m.

J hate shopping.

    I didn't always hate shopping.

I hate shopping now.

Everything I tried on felt tight and uncomfortable. The material was scratchy, or the stripes were ugly, or the color was the kind you'd have to wear sunglasses to behold. I had a hard time finding anything I would actually wear, even in a warehouse full of clothes.

Lisa filled a basket with new clothes for Anna. I've seen Anna's closet. She doesn't need a single thing.

First I carried a heaping pile of jeans and shorts into the dressing room. I tried on the first pair of jeans. They were too snug in the waist. I guess I've gone up a size (probably all those biscuits and pancakes I had to eat this summer). I looked at the rest of the pile and blinked my contacts back into place (they sure do blur a lot), and took the next pair of jeans from the stack. I knew, before pulling them on, that they wouldn't work either, but maybe I thought the universe still owed me a miracle.

I couldn't button them. And the Stonehenge in my throat started trembling.

The thing is, I knew I'd have to pass Dad, who waited right outside the dressing room, to either (a) hand the jeans, along with the words, "They didn't fit," to the employee guarding the dressing area or (b) return the jeans to the rack myself. Would Dad notice me walking back to the dressing room with a whole new stack of the same jeans and shorts, in a bigger size?

But I did it anyway. I put those jeans and shorts right back where I'd gotten them and picked up three more pairs of jeans, along with two pairs of shorts in my newly updated size.

Dad, of course, couldn't let me pass without saying something. This time he said, "Being picky, Tori?"

No, Dad, I just can't find anything that fits, if you want to know the truth.

I managed to plaster a smile on my face and say, "Just trying different styles to see what I like best."

Dad grunted. "Well, we don't have all day."

I was fully aware that we didn't have all day. My stomach was already rumbling.

And just like that, Dad once again made me feel smaller, boxed up, a tiny little insignificant thing whose preferences for clothes don't matter. Too bad that smallness didn't shave off a size.

The next stack of jeans fit better, which wasn't exactly what I wanted, but at least I didn't have to put them all back while Dad watched. I kept two, and both shorts, even though the only thing I could think when I looked in the mirror, my pale legs stretching what seemed like miles long, was how Dad would point out my "chicken legs" again.

After a while I felt so overwhelmed by the racks and racks of clothes, the choices stuffed together by size, that I just picked up the first shirts I liked and carried them to the dressing room. I ended up with six of them: three plain, one striped, one with flower designs, and one with lace detail on the back.

Add a pair of shoes, and it turns out you can get an entire week's wardrobe at the Nunya Superstore for Castoff Kids.

We piled our choices into the same basket where Lisa collected new clothes Anna didn't need, and before we walked to the register, she checked them all for flaws. She was so thorough, I felt glad she didn't make us parade in front of her so she could analyze a different kind of flaw: the Flaw of Unflattering Fit.

Maggie had to put back a shirt with a tiny hole in the hem, but it didn't take her long to find another in the exact same color, size, and style.

Dad took us out to a pizza buffet at Cici's. I only ate two pieces, because what good are new clothes if you can't wear them on the first day of school?

My stomach growled all the way back to Dad's house.

THINGS THAT HAVE CHICKEN LEGS

~~Twelve-year-old girls~~

Chickens

August 14, 8:06 p.m.

*T*his trip has seen more bad days than I really care to admit, but I'm pretty sure today took the gold medal among all the other Worst Days of The First Magnificent Summer with Dad.

I've been burning up for so long, it took me all day before I felt calm enough to write about it. My brain is still on fire, but I figure I need to get this down before I forget. Not that I ever will.

Here's what happened:

This morning Anna was bouncing around the kitchen like one of Ingram Junior High's fully inflated dodgeballs. (There aren't many; if you're lucky—and brave—enough to make it to the center line and grab one when Coach Finley blows her whistle, you better hold on to it the entire game, the better to bat balls away, and when it's just you and Shelly Thomas left on the court, you should throw it at her as hard as you possibly can, to epically end the game with a grunt and a smack. Hypothetically speaking.) Anna's voice collided with walls (and my head) and set my jaw into its most painful position—clenched. She moved from the table to the floor to Dad's lap to her plate. I kept waiting for Dad to say something, but he didn't say a thing. After all he's said about Mom and our manners and how he'd probably do a better job raising us, he can't even manage to keep his new daughter at the table.

Maybe that's unfair. He's not usually the one who keeps her contained. Lisa is. I don't know where Lisa was at that particular moment. Just like I thought it would, my memory has fogged a few of the details. I see Dad, I see myself, I see Anna being completely and utterly obnoxious.

Even now I can't imagine doing the same thing she was doing when I was three without Dad smacking the backs of my legs or stinging me with words. Probably both.

My throat burned, and I tried to ignore her as long as I could, and just when I was reaching my breaking point, Dad shoved away from the table and opened the pantry, rummaging around for something. The distraction he provided was a miracle. And, yes, my standards for miracles have plummeted significantly.

He dragged out the dog bowl and filled it up for Heidi, then called Heidi inside.

"Heidi!" Anna cooed in her little-girl voice. I tried not to let the sickness in my stomach erupt out my mouth at Anna petting and draping herself over our dog like Heidi had always been hers. At least Anna was still for two seconds.

Dad slid from the room without another glance back at any of us. And I guess Lisa *was* in the kitchen, because she plays pretty heavily into this next part, although I can't remember where she was standing.

What happened next seemed to unfold in slow motion. Anna moving from Heidi's back to Heidi's front, reaching into the food bowl, Heidi snapping with a growl (not a ferocious one, just a warning one), Lisa scooping Anna up, screaming. Dad rushed back into the room. Jack and I were standing now (so Jack was there too), Maggie was covering her ears (so Maggie was there), Lisa was shouting, "Heidi bit Anna, she bit Anna!" pointing to Anna's hand. Even from where I was standing, I could see it was the smallest scratch in the history of the world's scratches, no blood to be seen, but Lisa was completely hysterical.

I glanced at Heidi. Her tail curled between her legs like she knew she'd done something wrong and regretted it. If dogs can regret past actions. She didn't meet anyone's eyes but stared at the floor like she understood everything Lisa said.

"We'll have to get rid of her." Lisa's voice was still hysterical, bordering on a maniacal screech.

What did she mean, get rid of her? Like, give her away or like . . .

Also, what a stupid, stupid reason to get rid of a dog. Heidi did what any dog would do if a little girl reached into the food bowl while the dog was eating. I'm not a dog expert, but I still know animals are, in general, protective of their food. Especially an animal kept in a backyard, away from her humans all day, and fed once, maybe twice a day, at varying times. Maybe dogs are like Jack and me (Jack more so than me, but still me). Maybe they need stability and predictability and the kind of dinner that's laid out at the exact same time every evening so you can look at the clock and think, *It's four thirty now, that means an hour until dinner, I don't need a snack when it's only an hour until dinner.*

Maybe it was none of my business, and maybe it was the wrong thing to do (I did promise to tell the truth about myself in these pages too), but I inserted myself into the conversation, pronto.

"What do you mean, get rid of her?" I said.

Lisa looked at me like she hadn't heard. But she shrieked at Dad, "We'll have to give her away!" She pressed

Anna's face into her shoulder. Anna had not stopped crying, probably because Lisa had not stopped shrieking.

It didn't even draw blood. It wasn't a vicious action. But how do you explain that to someone who's hysterical?

I tried.

"Give her away for—"

"What happened?" Dad completely interrupted me, which, let's just say, is extremely rude. I was in the middle of saying something important and was *about* to tell him exactly what happened. He didn't look at me, though. In fact, he didn't look at any of the calm people in the room (which amounted to me, Jack, and Maggie). He looked at Hysterical Lisa.

Anna, by this point, was crying so loud, it almost rivaled Lisa's repeated shriek. "She bit Anna!" Lisa shrieked again. (See, in writing you're supposed to only say "said" after dialogue, but Lisa didn't just *say* the words, she *shrieked* them. She may even have gone up a step from shriek; she may have screamed/squealed/squawked. All three of them together.) She pointed an accusatory finger at Heidi, who hung her head even lower.

Dad grabbed Heidi's collar and dragged her toward the back door. "Bad dog," he said in the kind of voice that could freeze boiling water. For a minute I was afraid for Heidi, but he slammed back through the door and closed it behind him. I could hear Heidi whimpering, and it filled me with the kind of rage that moves feet and tongues, both.

"She didn't even get to eat!" I shouted. (Yes, I shouted oh so disrespectfully. I could see the rage burning a fire across Dad's face. It was way bigger than mine. I really shouldn't have raced so easily into a place I didn't belong. But it gets worse.)

My next words came out in a bonfire of anger and fear. "Heidi never would have scratched Anna if Anna hadn't been stupid enough to mess with her food."

The words seemed to hang in the air, all my poisonous hatred soaking them. All the breath shook out of my lungs as I realized what I'd done. The kitchen stilled, like even the universe's molecules knew I'd said the worst words I could possibly say.

I wished I could take them back. But the thing about spoken words is you can't erase them or scratch them out or cover them with permanent marker until you can't see them anymore. They stick in the air, pointing their fingers toward you and turning on a neon sign that blinks "Doomed."

I knew I was doomed. I should have expected what came next.

It didn't take Dad long to cross the kitchen, lift a hand, and hit me so hard across the cheek, I heard my neck crack and saw pulsing black dots at the corners of my vision. I always thought it was a literary device authors used when they said the world spun for someone who'd been hit, but it really did spin. I grabbed the wall to steady myself. Dad's eyes flashed like green bolts of lightning when he said, "Don't you ever call your sister stupid again." He shoved out the back door, Heidi's food bowl in hand. I heard him say, "You'll eat outside from now on," and maybe that means he'll keep her, that he knows he can't give her away for something so stupid. Maybe that means speaking up saved a little piece of the world today. I don't know. It was hard to think. It still is.

And it doesn't matter.

The whole thing was stupid.

Anna was stupid.

Lisa was stupid.

I hate them.

She's not my sister.

She will never, ever, ever be my sister.

Those are all the words I swallowed after Dad hit me. I folded them deep down inside myself, and it's only now, when Dad's gone to a bar and Lisa's somewhere in her bedroom and Anna's sleeping and Heidi's who knows where, that I let them back out.

There's another piece to the day that bothers me. The

last thing I saw before I scrambled from the kitchen to my room—not my room, Anna's room, where I'm staying as Dad's unwelcome guest—was Dad standing in front of Heidi with a thick roll of newspaper raised high, ugly words ripping from his throat. "You are a bad dog. I won't keep a bad dog around." I moved away before I could see what he was going to do with the newspaper roll. I knew.

My hands started shaking, and my vision went black again for a second. I didn't want the memory to come back, but memories have minds of their own.

Dad used to hit us, with the belt he still wears. I tried to bury that part of the story, because while some people think hope is this uncrushable thing with feathers, I know feathers are pretty fragile. I wanted hope to have a chance this summer. You know?

Dad didn't use the same words he yelled at Heidi while he lashed us, but he may as well have. He didn't keep us around, did he?

I hate him. I wish he wasn't our dad. I wish he'd never brought us here for the summer.

I can't wait to go home.

If this is the last summer Dad ever brings us to Ohio, I'll be glad. So, so glad.

I can't believe I missed him.

I can't believe I thought we could impress him—*I could*

impress him. (Maybe the handprint on my face will impress him, I don't know.)

I can't believe I convinced myself things would be different now than they were back then.

Now that I've written all that, I don't ever want to see it again. Memory closed. Don't come back.

In three days, we'll be heading home. Surely I can survive three more days.

I never thought I'd be so relieved to leave Dad behind.

GOLD
(Becoming)

It is only by putting it into words that I make it whole;
this wholeness means that it has lost its power to hurt me;
it gives me, perhaps because by doing so I take away the
pain, a great delight to put the severed parts together.
—Virginia Woolf

Period (**noun**): an important word—spoken or unspoken—added to the end of a statement to imply that no further discussion (observing, commenting, arguing, refuting) is possible or welcome, as in: That's the end of the matter. That's that. I am right and you are wrong and you should not try to prove otherwise.

Some people have a habit—or maybe it's a talent—for delivering every sentence in such a way that observing/commenting/arguing/refuting is completely and utterly discouraged. For example, when Dad speaks to anyone—to Lisa: "Go get my milk for me, honey." (maybe he thinks the "honey" added to the end sweetens the order); to Anna: "Sit down and eat your food." (which he didn't say and which might have prevented everything that happened on August 14); to us: "Get your suitcases, kids, it's time to go." (along with the "Thank God it's finally over" you could see all over his face)—it is with an understood period at the end of his statements.

You should be ashamed of yourself. Period. You are disappointing. Period. You will never write again. Period.

Other people are born such cowards, they cannot utilize this form of speech. And so the definitive statement I want to say (I am Victoria Reeves, and I will write as long as I have a pen. Period.) remains trapped behind whatever rock wall now lives in my throat (which is here to stay). Period.

*J*ust when you think it can't get worse, the universe decides to show you you're outrageously wrong.

Surviving three more days with Dad and The Replacements didn't seem all that hard yesterday, before The Worst Thing That Could Possibly Happen happened.

I also thought The Worst Thing That Could Possibly Happen was getting my first period one thousand miles away from Mom, but it turns out I was wrong about that, too.

And then I thought The Worst Thing That Could Possibly Happen was watching Dad with Heidi yesterday, blurting something I shouldn't have said, feeling his slap sting my face. Wrong. Again.

I shouldn't be writing in this journal. I shouldn't be writing in anything ever again, according to Dad. I shouldn't even think about picking up a pen or a pencil because the world does not need my words.

That's a direct quote.

But I dug this journal out from the pile of new clothes in my suitcase, and I'm hiding away three blocks down, in the shade of a tree, where Dad can't see me. I snuck the journal out in my shirt, pressed up against my back, and that's how I'll sneak it back in. I just needed to write.

You'll understand in a second. (You've probably blocked out this memory, if you're smart.)

There was no beating on a pot to wake us up this morning, no Dad's voice telling us to get out of bed, don't be lazy, don't waste the whole day. There was no sound at all, and I guess that's what woke me.

Or maybe it was the stagnant nature of the air inside the house, like everything held its breath, waiting for an axe to swing out and take off my head. (And it would. Metaphorically speaking.)

I wish I'd stayed in bed, but, looking at that objectively, it wouldn't have been a solution. Dad would have found me eventually. Unless I'd started walking in the direction of Texas, if I even knew which direction that was (which I don't). Maybe I should have run.

It wouldn't have made a difference. Nothing would have.

So now I sit here, sweating in the shade of a tree (I don't know what kind; I was never good at identifying trees, and this is foreign territory, Ohio instead of Texas), about to write about The Worst Thing That Could Possibly Happen.

Maybe I should just forget it. Maybe I should swipe it from my memory store like Dad's words didn't add more purple bruises to my cheek that will definitely be yellowing by the time I start seventh grade. Maybe it's better that way.

But how else to explain the gaps in these journals?

So this morning I woke with my shoulders so tense, they must have been telling me something bad was afoot, but I didn't listen. I sat up, shook them out, and reached under my pillow for my notebooks, the way I do every morning.

But my notebooks were gone.

The panic is hard to describe now that I'm done with it. But it felt like all the other panic attacks put together, except this one was much, much worse. My mouth became the Atacama Desert, which Sarah's grandmother, who used to be a geography teacher, once told me is the driest place on earth. My arms and legs felt like maybe they'd gained a hundred pounds while I was sleeping, and my chest went cold, hot, cold, numb, hot, cold, hot, cold, numb, like it couldn't decide which extreme it wanted to be.

Where are my notebooks? clanged in my head, over and over again.

But I knew.

Still, I tore the room apart, looking for them. I stripped the bed, pulled everything out from underneath the bed, even picked up the mattress with my hundred-pounds-heavier arms.

My notebooks did not turn up.

I raced downstairs and stopped right outside the kitchen. Maggie was already sitting at the table, but Jack was nowhere to be found. I wasn't sure if I wanted to make my presence known yet, so I stood there for a minute, listening to Dad and Lisa yelling, hardly breathing. I pressed the back of my head against the wall and closed my eyes. I don't know if I was praying or just trying to make myself invisible. Maybe a little of both.

"Her mother needs to know," Lisa said. My heart hammered so hard I thought (1) they might hear it and figure out I was there, lurking, and (2) it would gallop right out of my chest and across the kitchen floor so they could squash it and turn their anger on the heartless me. But no one even looked in my direction.

For a second I thought—hoped—maybe they were talking about something Maggie had done. She was, after all, sitting at the table like a kid in trouble.

It was wishful thinking.

"You've really done it now," Jack whispered behind me. I didn't even dignify his words with a response, but my whole body went cold.

And I knew. I *knew*. I knew even before I heard Dad say, "Let me see that," before I heard the torturous silence, before the ripping of paper.

Dad said a bunch of bad words I refuse to record. Just trust me when I say it was a lot. Then he said, "Hand me the phone."

I must have gasped, because someone shoved me into shadows. Maybe it was Jack, maybe it was my own self, trying to protect what secrecy I had left to me.

They read my personal journals.

They read my personal journals.

They read my personal journals.

I had no secret places left. I folded myself up so small, I thought maybe I could stay invisible forever.

Wednesday, Thursday, Friday. That's all I had to survive. Wednesday, Thursday, Friday, Wednesday, Thursday, Friday. The days repeated in my head as I waited for Mom to answer the phone call.

Finally, Dad said, "Connie? We need to talk about your daughter."

Which one which one which one

I knew which one.

Dad's voice didn't stay calm for long. He called Mom a terrible name, said she was raising the kind of daughter who writes terrible things about people, moved back into calling her more terrible names, shifted so easily into calling me terrible names.

Brat. Bad-tempered. Another *B* word I refuse to write.

The kind of person who writes trash about people.

The kind of person who writes lies about people.

The kind of person who writes what the world doesn't need: trash and lies.

Maybe that's not what he said, but that's what I heard. And now I don't have enough time left to change his mind.

Every one of his words got caught in my throat. I choked and crawled to the doorway, where I could see Lisa holding my journals—my personal journals!—in her pasty white hands with the kind of look on her face that says she's pretty sure she smells the worst thing in the collection of Worst Smelly Things. (I give all my votes to Jack's burps after he's had pizza, which smell like three-week-old pizza took a bath in vomit.) She looked so outraged, I wasn't sure I'd have a place to sleep tonight—which is just fine by me. I'll sleep under the stars, somewhere on the road back to Texas. If they'll just point the way.

Maybe Dad will take us home early, and I won't have

Wednesday and Thursday to survive before Friday and its promise of seeing Mom.

Dad's words faded after a while—"I can't believe you let her write such god-awful things. . . ." "She's not getting these journals back. . . ." "She needs to understand she can't say these kinds of things about people." He talked in circles, round and round while the roaring sound swelled in my ears and wrapped around my chest, squeezing. I couldn't breathe at all. I thought I might die right there, and for a minute, I have to admit, I thought it might be better. For everyone. For the world that doesn't need my words.

But there's so much more living to do, and so many more words to write, and . . .

I guess Mom asked to talk to me, because the next thing I knew, Dad yanked me up out of the corner in the same rough way he'd yanked Heidi out of the kitchen yesterday. Maybe panic and terror make you weightless, because he didn't even grunt with effort, and I flopped right where he wanted me to go, nothing more than a worn-out rag doll. He shoved the phone into my hand. "Your mother wants to talk to you," he said, and he took a step back and folded his arms and looked at me like he'd never met a person so disgusting in his life.

I ruined everything with my words. They were supposed to fix things.

I didn't say anything for a minute, but I guess Mom could hear my breathing, because she said, "Well, your dad read your diary, sweetie."

It's a journal, and I've told her that a million times, but I didn't correct her. I just said, "Yeah," and it came out so small and squeaky, you would have thought Mom was talking to a mouse.

"I'm so sorry, sweetie," Mom said, and I almost wished she hadn't said it, because that's when the tears started falling. I felt so ashamed that I'd written those awful words yesterday. I felt so ashamed that someone had read them, even though they weren't supposed to. I felt so ashamed for the way I felt.

I felt ashamed for being me.

Those words weren't supposed to be for anyone else, they were supposed to stay mine and only mine forever. Why didn't I think about the possibility of someone reading them? Because I never had to think about it with Mom—she let me write and never, ever asked to see my journals. She believed my words belonged to me until I was ready to let someone see them—if ever.

How did this happen?

"I know it's been hard there," Mom said. "And I'm so, so sorry."

She was crying too.

"We'll have to talk about this when you get home."

"Okay," I said. By this point, I was shaking with sobs, and you could barely understand me.

"Don't cry, Tori," Mom said. "Everything will be okay."

I wish her words had been true. I wish they could have protected me from the wrath I knew was waiting for me the minute I hung up the phone and had to face Dad and Lisa and the words I'd recorded in a private journal they read without my consent.

I wanted to keep Mom on the phone, so I said, "You'll be there to pick us up?"

"Of course, sweetie. I'll be waiting."

Dad folded his arms across his chest, reminding me that he was right there listening in on my conversation in the same way he'd listened in on my private thoughts by reading my private journal.

"I love you," Mom said.

"I love you too."

The last thing Mom said to me was, "He shouldn't have read your journal, Tori. Whatever else you hear today, you should know that."

I guess Mom knew what was coming too.

I hung up, the hot breath of Dad's rage sweeping over

my face. My hand lifted, almost involuntarily, to the cheek he smacked yesterday.

"Your sister found this," Dad said, holding up the corner of my turquoise journal like he couldn't stand to touch it, like it was the breeding ground of some deadly plague, like it would maybe end the world if left to its own devices.

Who knew private journals could be so powerful?

I looked at Maggie, but she shook her head. So he was talking about Anna. My anger was so fierce and hot, it surprised me.

How dare she touch my private journals. I thought about Mom's words. *He shouldn't have read your journal. Whatever else you hear today, you should know that.*

"No one's supposed to read my journals unless I let them," I said.

It was a stupid thing to say. Dad slapped me, harder even than yesterday. And on the same cheek. I thought my skin might burn right up in the torch of that sting.

Lisa moved into the doorway, her mouth set in a perfect straight line—it was not a flattering look, but I don't think she was concerned about beauty in the moment—and said, "I found Anna reading the journal."

And I don't know what to tell you. I had a moment of insanity, and I laughed. "She's three. She can't read."

Yes. Those ignorant words actually came out of my mouth.

Dad slapped me again, in the same exact spot. My cheek felt like it might fall off. I'm pretty sure I took a step back, away from him. Maybe I even glared at him. I don't know.

I think I can imagine how it happened: The journal slipped out from under my pillow, Anna couldn't resist touching something that was mine, she opened it in the middle of the floor and pretended to read, Lisa found her like that, maybe saw her name, couldn't resist reading, and, like the tattletale she is, took it straight to Dad.

I should have buried the journal in my suitcase and zipped it shut. Anna has trouble with zippers.

This next part really pains me to report.

Dad opened the offending journal and started ripping out pages, tearing them in halves and quarters, eighths, sixteenths, and tossing them on the ground in flutters of white papery snow. He held up the purple journal, the one with all my fiction stories.

"No!" I shouted, and lunged for it.

Dad smacked me so hard I flew backward.

"You think you'll ever write again?" Dad said, his eyes blazing at me. "Not in this house. If I had my way, you'd never write again." He tore out every single one of those pages, ripped them like he did the ones in my journal, and tossed them on the floor, white pieces covering the yellowing linoleum.

All those words, lost.

I felt so sick, I thought I might vomit right there.

"I will not have a daughter who writes such awful things about people," Dad said around clenched-tight teeth. Rip, rip, rip. "I will not." Rip, rip, rip. "You think you're so wise, with all your words." Rip, rip, rip. "But all you are is a hateful little girl." Rip, rip, rip. "The world doesn't need your hateful words." Rip, rip, rip. "You will not write again while you are under this roof." Rip, rip, rip.

When he finished tearing out every page, when all the scraps finished fluttering to the floor, when my breath turned to gasping heaves, Dad said, "Now. Clean it up."

And I gladly did. Because I thought maybe, maybe, maybe, I could save something from the wreckage.

But the paper pieces were too small, and there were too many of them, mixed and scattered and out of place.

I scraped them into a pile instead and started depositing handfuls into the trash can Dad kicked into the room. My eyes were too blurry to even see the words or try to put the pages back together, but they weren't too blurry to see Jack and Maggie, on their hands and knees, gathering scraps along with me.

And now you have the full account of The Worst Thing That Could Possibly Happen. Technically, I did not write any of this while under Dad's roof. That said, I don't know if I'll be able to write again before we get back home.

So happy First Magnificent Summer with Dad, Victoria Reeves.

August 17, 12:03 a.m.

*T*oday is the day we'll leave for Texas.

I can't sleep. I haven't had a chance to write about something else that happened. No, it wasn't another Worst Thing That Could Possibly Happen, although this wouldn't have happened if The Worst Thing That Could Possibly Happen hadn't happened. If that makes sense. I'm tired, and I'm curled up by the only window in Anna's room, trying to write by moonlight.

Tonight, before I lay down, I put my hand under my pillow, probably out of habit, since I'm usually sliding a notebook under the pillow. (I hide this notebook in my suitcase now, under all my new clothes, zipped closed.) And do you know what I found under my pillow?

I found all the pages from my other notebooks, the ones

Dad ripped out and tore up. They were all taped together. Whole. You could read them! Some were missing middles or edges or whole lines, but you could read them! Stories, poems, essays. Journal entries. I didn't lose my words. At least not all of them.

I was so happy I didn't even care that another person read my journal.

Sometimes Jack's the best brother in the world.

(He was asleep when I went to tell him this exact thing, but I left him a gift under his pillow too.)

THE BEST AND THE WORST: A PARADOX

(for Jack)
It must have taken him hours
to put my journal back together—
  Jack's the best

It only took him seconds
to call our beloved
Which One's the Grossest game
a stupid game—
  Jack's the worst

How did he even figure out
which piece went where?
  Jack's the best

How did he know what would be
the ultimate gut punch?

> Jack's the worst

I imagine he snuck back
into the kitchen while Dad
wasn't paying attention

> (probably watching one of his soap
>
> > operas)

and pulled out every
tiny piece of paper he could find
from the trash—

> Jack's the best

I imagine he thought he was
something special when he decided
he was too old to play games
with fuzzy food—

> Jack's the worst

He risked everything
we've ever wanted

> (Dad's affection and approval
>
> and blah blah blah)

to rescue something that means

everything to me—
      Jack's the best

All in all,
I think there's more of the
      best
than the
      worst

And I guess that's what is
so surprising about
brothers

And why even when you think
they can't possibly get any
      crueler ghastlier rottener
you realize that even at their smelliest
      you love them so so much

*D*ad hasn't said a word to us in the car. He silently watched us pack our things in the back and climbed in the front seat. Lisa and Anna and Devon stayed home this time, probably because of me. Maybe Dad's mad about that—they can't stand to be around me.

I forgot to mention in this morning's first entry that he called Mom again last night and told her he'd meet her two hundred miles closer to Ohio. He'd pay for her gas. I guess he's so ready to be rid of us, he can't be bothered to take us all the way to the original meeting place.

Well, the feeling's mutual.

I rub my chest. It's felt tight and uncomfortable since we left.

Jack and Maggie sit in the second seat, where Anna and

Devon were on the way to Ohio. I went ahead and climbed in the Way Back so I would (1) be as far away from Dad and his hands as possible and (2) have a chance of sneaking this journal out of my shirt and writing in it (which is what I'm doing now. It's tricky, though. I have to make sure I'm looking up every few seconds so Dad doesn't catch on to what I'm doing. And I can't write for long). At least the windows are rolled down this time.

We left early, before the sun was up. Lisa hugged us all— even me—and told us she'd see us next summer. I knew there wouldn't be a next summer, but I nodded anyway.

Heidi was nowhere around, so we couldn't tell her goodbye. I hope they find her a good home, instead of . . . well, I don't even want to think about the alternative.

I've tried sleeping in the Way Back, since I have the seat to myself, and I hardly slept at all last night, but my throat's too tight. All Dad's words are like fire ants stinging me. Maybe I really shouldn't write again. Maybe the world really doesn't need my words. Maybe my words hurt people.

I don't want to hurt people.

We make the necessary stops along the way—a few times to use the bathroom, once to eat. Dad didn't bring a cooler this time, and we sat around a table at Cracker Barrel, saying practically nothing. Even though it was lunchtime, I ordered biscuits and gravy and ate them while Dad pretended I didn't exist. He talked to Jack mostly, every now and then saying something to Maggie. I felt like Casper the Friendly Ghost, watching the world around me and wondering if I'd ever be able to join it as more than a ghost. Maybe that's the real power of my words: they disappeared, so I did too.

The miles peel away, but I don't feel any kind of excitement. I am Stonehenge. A girl made of stone. A girl overtaken by the boulders that keep her from speaking.

A girl finally made as small as Dad wanted me to be.

August 17, 6:34 p.m.

*W*e watched Dad drive away until we couldn't see him anymore, and I knew it would probably be the last time.

The First Magnificent Summer is over now.

Already, my memory has started constructing a better version of Dad than this summer showed me. Maybe that's the way it's supposed to be. Maybe that's how you survive your less-than-magnificent summers. Maybe that's how you learn to forgive.

I'm just not completely ready yet. To forgive, I mean. And maybe that's okay too.

When we turned into the parking lot at the Shell station, Mom was leaning against the hood of our Ford Escort with the hatchback, gray and rusty in places. Memaw stood beside her, two inches shorter, the two of them watching the highway. I don't know if I've ever been happier to see them both.

Mom stood up straighter when Dad pulled in, gravel popping under the tires. He parked beside her and bolted out of the driver's seat like he couldn't wait to get out of there.

In their excitement to see Mom, Jack and Maggie forgot to pull the seat forward so I could climb out of the Way Back. So they had already greeted Mom by the time I stepped onto the gravel, and her eyes were all mine. I could only feel them on me; everything was too blurry. I blinked fast to fix my contacts.

I didn't want Dad to see me cry.

Mom pulled me into her arms and held me for what seemed like a long time. "I'm so glad you're home," she said, and my breath caught. I nodded against her, because I couldn't trust my words or my voice. "I'm so sorry about what happened there at the end." She said the words so quietly, I knew they were only for me.

I nodded against her again.

I'll wait to tell her that Dad threw away every page of my stories, every record that this summer existed at all— but that Jack saved the day and patched them up.

Dad set our suitcases on the ground. "Can you pop

the trunk?" He sounded annoyed and hurried, like he was already tired of our tearful reunion. Mom moved to the trunk. She looked beautiful in her red shirt and jeans, her black curls framing her cheeks. I wondered if seeing her made Dad think about all he gave up when he left.

He turned to Jack first. He hugged us all and kissed the tops of our heads. He had more words for some than others. (I bet you can guess who got the fewest.) He didn't apologize for what he did, but neither did I.

If I had my way, you would never write again.

Somewhere in all the ruminating (the English language has so many delightful words!), the *if I had my way* got lost. It became, *You will never write again.*

Almost like he knew what I was thinking, Dad said to Jack and Maggie, "You'll write me some letters? I'd like to have some letters from you."

Would he? Or are those just more empty words that mean nothing? I couldn't tell by looking at him. His eyes were hooded and closed. Because of what I did or because of who he is?

"You too, Tori."

Was he apologizing?

My words got caught in my throat. *My name is Victoria.*

Dad climbed back in his car, rolled down the window, and said, "I love you kids. Can't wait until next summer."

He didn't look at us when he said that, but he did when he said, "I'll call on Saturday."

That was the only time he looked back on his way home to The Replacements.

He forgot to give Mom the gas money.

Mom let us watch him until the Suburban disappeared, and then she said, "Come on. Let's go home."

I felt like I was splitting in two.

August 17, 8:42 p.m.

$\mathcal{W}$e stopped for supper at a place somewhere between Waco and Houston, where they served fried chicken right along with roast and potatoes. I ate more than I ate all summer.

When we got back in the car, Memaw handed us each a package.

"What's this?" Jack said. Something stuck out of his pocket, a corner of a folded-up paper. It looked like the poem I left under his pillow.

In spite of everything, it made me smile.

"A little gift from your mom and me," Memaw said.

I knew it was probably mostly from Memaw. Mom doesn't usually have money for gifts that aren't tied to a birthday or special holiday.

Jack ripped off the brown paper wrapping his. Inside the small box were Jack's favorite books in the world: Stephen King's Dark Tower trilogy. Maggie got a new cross-stitch book (Memaw taught her how last summer) and a collection of thread and material. I held my package for a minute, my heart sliding up into my throat.

Memaw watched me. She said, "Are you going to open yours, Victoria?" I lifted my head. Memaw smiled at me. She has the same shade of brown eyes as Mom, but hers are folded up into more wrinkles.

Mom must have told her I wanted to drop my nickname now that I'm getting older. My eyes burned, and I blinked hard. Those stupid contacts. I held the package one more minute before I tore a corner of the wrapping.

Inside was a set of the most beautiful pens I'd ever seen. And a brand-new journal. This one had a lock and two tiny silver keys dangling from the clasp.

"So you can write," Mom said, "and not worry about who might see it."

You'll never write again.

I can't write.

But what am I doing now?

I *can* write. Dad doesn't have the last word.

You'll never write again.

My shoulders slumped, and I shook my head. The words

came spilling out. "He told me I shouldn't write anymore. That my words are dangerous. They hurt people." I didn't care that Jack and Maggie were staring at me and that my words were all tangled around tears.

Mom smacked her hand against the steering wheel, and Memaw put a hand on Mom's arm and turned around in her seat to face me and said, "Don't you ever let someone tell you who to be, Victoria. Don't you ever let someone tell you what you can and cannot do. Don't ever let them make you feel ashamed for your passions or your opinions or for being you." Her voice rose with every sentence, fervor filling her words like they were tumblers of her favorite beverage—Dr Pepper.

Memaw divorced her husband twenty-one years ago, after nineteen years of marriage. She's lived all by herself all these years. If anyone does what she wants, it's Memaw.

I'm glad I have Memaw.

Mom took a deep breath and blew it out loudly. I could tell she was trying to arrange her words in an intentional, careful way. She finally said, "Your dad never should have read your journal, Tori." She paused. "Victoria." Another pause. "But you have to understand that your dad is also not in charge of your life. He can't keep you locked up inside some box of his own making. He doesn't get to say who you are or who you'll become." She glanced in the rearview mirror and met my eyes. "No one has that kind of power over you, Victoria. Not unless you let them."

I guess Mom learned a thing or two when she and Dad split up.

My voice sounded small when I said, "He threw away all my stories." Jack shifted beside me.

"So you'll write more," Memaw said.

"He said the world doesn't need my words," I said. I didn't mention the slap. The multiple slaps. I don't know why. I touched my cheek. I swear the skin there still stung.

Mom cursed. I felt my eyes widen. Mom doesn't ever curse.

"Does the world need your words, Victoria?" Mom said.

I don't know. Does it?

Mom asked it again, her voice louder this time. "Does the world need your words, Victoria?"

"I don't know. I guess," I managed to say.

"The answer is yes," Memaw said. "It does." She shifted to face me again, and I could feel Mom's eyes still on me in the rearview mirror. The lights of passing cars illuminated their faces every few seconds, before they were cast in darkness again.

"So show it you have something to say," Mom said.

I traced the words imprinted on the front of the journal Mom and Memaw gave me and thought about what they meant for a long time.

August 17, 9:05 p.m.

I guess I should tell you what's imprinted on the front of the journal Mom and Memaw gave me, since, if you're reading this, you're not reading it in my new journal. I'm saving it for what I'm tentatively calling The Magnificent School Year That Is Seventh Grade. (I might have to find another adjective besides "magnificent," since that one seems to be slightly cursed—that's why it's a tentative title.)

It's a quote from Simone de Beauvoir, a French novelist who wrote all kinds of books that Mom said made lots of people mad. (I had to ask Mom who she was. I thought she was a he at first!)

The quote is from her book *All Said and Done*, which was published in 1972. Mom says she'll let me read it as soon as I turn sixteen.

It says, "For a woman, the point is not to prove herself as a woman but to be acknowledged as a 'whole,' 'complete' human being."

On the first page of the journal, Memaw wrote, "Nolite te bastardes carborundorum." It's a line from Margaret Atwood's *The Handmaid's Tale*, which Mom also said she'd let me read when I turn sixteen. (I've got a list going, don't worry. I won't forget.) Memaw says it means "Don't let the bastards grind you down." (She also said "bastard" isn't really a bad word, but I'm not so sure. I wrote it anyway.)

I added two quotes of my own, one from Harriet Beecher Stowe: "I feel now that the time is come when even a woman or a child who can speak a word for freedom and humanity is bound to speak." and the other from Virginia Woolf: "No need to hurry. No need to sparkle. No need to be anybody but oneself."

I stared at those quotes for a long, long time before I finally pulled out one of those fancy pens, opened my old journal (because, like I said, the new one is reserved for something else), and showed the world that I do have something to say.

*P*ERIOD

1a

Sometimes I get emotional and I cry. Period.

1b

I am not a coward. Period.

2

I don't like camping. Period.

I don't like swimming in lakes. Period.

3

I am tall. Period.

I take up space. Period.

I will not be small. Period.

4

I don't always have nice thoughts, but I do
    mostly keep them to myself. Period.
I should be able to write what I want to write.
    Period.
I will guard my words. Period.
But I will also give my words. Period.

5

I am father-less. Period.
I am mother-full. Period.
I am not defined by what I don't have (for
    example: a father). Period.
I might not ever see my dad again. Period.
I will be okay. Period.

6

Mom says I can wear black mascara next year.
    Period.
She says I grew up this summer. Period.
She says we all have our secret lives with
    thoughts and opinions, and they should
    remain secret for as long as we want them
    to. Period.
I guess that applies to Dad, too. Period.

Maybe I'll never figure him out or win him
over or repair what's been broken, and
maybe that's not the point. Period.
Growing up isn't about fitting in or making
yourself smaller or trying to fold yourself
into this perfect version of who you think
you should be, it's about stretching into
who you are, even if it means leaving some
people, like your dad, behind. Period.

7

I wanted my dad to love me. Period.
He does, in his own way. Period.
But I don't need him to. Period.
Because I was born, and that's the only
necessary requirement for deserving love.
Period.
I will not wait for my dad—or anyone else—to
tell me how I should live my life or who I
should be. Period.
I am who I am. Period.
My name is Victoria. Period.

*W*e're finally home.

I'm back in my bed, in my bedroom, curled up under familiar covers with a familiar flashlight, writing these final words to complete this summer's story.

This might be "The First Magnificent Summer with Dad" or it might be "The First and Last Magnificent Summer with Dad." (Technically, "magnificent" is a totally inaccurate description of this summer, but that title was not a tentative one and I've decided to honor the overly optimistic Victoria I was thirty days ago.)

Either way, it IS The First Magnificent Summer of Victoria Reeves. And I'll be okay.

I have my words.

And the world needs them.

August 21, 12:03 p.m.

*Y*ou wanted a happy ending.

Yeah. Me too.

But the thing I'm learning is that relationships don't always turn out the way you want them to. Sometimes a brother gets home from a summer with his dad and he picks up that trumpet (he's a little better now, but it's still WAY TOO LOUD, Jack, and I would really like to enjoy the rest of my quiet summer. Emphasis on the quiet) because music is his therapy, and you think, *He really is the worst,* even though he taped all those ripped pages back together and thanks to him you didn't lose all your best stories (probably not your best, but I'm trying to make a point). Sometimes your mom says, "I have someone I want you kids to meet," and you feel that tiny little jolt—disappointment, sadness, maybe a little bit of anger—because hope is like a clingy little sticker burr you thought you put in the trash can until you're walking around barefoot (okay, maybe you're stomping because you don't really want to meet anyone new, you're not sure your heart can take it), and it splits your foot in half again.

Sometimes your dad rips up your words, says some awful things, and doesn't call or write to apologize.

People change. But not always the way you want or in ways you can even see.

A happy ending isn't always loose ends all tied up perfectly neat and clean. Sure, we'd like them to be, but that's not life. I may be young, but I already know that.

Happy endings sometimes look like Maggie's hair after she's spent the day running around outside like a wild child racing the wind—standing up in every direction, tangled so marvelously you'll never get a brush through it.

Not everything gets fixed. And you can't wait around expecting everything to get fixed when you don't really have control over that.

You can't control other people. You only control you.

The happiest endings are the ones where you learn no one—not a mom or a dad or other people you know or don't know—can dictate who you can be or shrink your importance to the world.

So I guess this is my happy ending: I learned to stand on my own.

I am Victoria Reeves. A little weird, hopefully a lot funny, and completely, wholly myself.

Author's Note

Families are all complicated in their own ways. They are made up of real, complicated people, who came from their own complicated families. Some dads never learned how to be good dads. Some moms never learned how to be good moms.

So parents sometimes leave. They walk out and never look back. Maybe they do it before we're old enough to even notice or know any better. Maybe they stick around long enough to say awful things or hurt us in all the hidden places.

Either way, it's a deep, massive wound they leave when they walk away.

If you are one of the 18.5 million children in the United States living in a single-parent household—and the millions more worldwide—there is something important I want you to know:

It has nothing to do with you.

When a parent we love leaves us, it's so easy to go over and over and over all the things we did or said or didn't do or say, to try to find a reason for their leaving. We could have been more obedient or helpful or agreeable. We could have made better grades. We could have cried less or smiled more. We could have been someone completely different.

That wound our parent left whispers all kinds of lies. *Not good enough*, it says. *Not worthy of love*, it says. *Worthless*, it says.

He would have stayed if you'd been a better person, it says.

Here's the other important thing I want you to know:

You deserve to be loved simply because you're you.

Not because you make perfect grades or write interesting stories or run the fastest mile on the track team or are the best singer or can play the clarinet like a professional or you know all the right answers to the most important tests.

It's important enough to say again:

You deserve to be loved simply because you're you.

And who you are is magnificent.

Those of us with broken stories don't all get happy endings. Moms sometimes stay gone a long, long time. Dads sometimes don't come back. They don't even remember our birthday or know our favorite color or have any idea who our friends are or what we dream of doing in our lives.

But these things have a way of working out in the end.

I survived my own broken story.

I believe you'll be okay too.

ᴀᴄᴋɴᴏᴡʟᴇᴅɢᴍᴇɴᴛꜱ

This book took years to write. I wrote the first draft in prose. The second draft morphed into a novel in verse, the third draft back into prose, the fourth draft back into poetry. Then it shapeshifted into a journal story with poetry asides.

Obviously, it was not an easy story to write. It took a long time to write because it was a difficult story. But it also took a long time to write because I wrote most of its later drafts while trying to monitor six children through remote learning during a global pandemic.

There were many, many people who helped me have the strength, the fortitude, and the ability to see this story through to publication.

First and foremost, a huge thank-you goes out to Ben, who has never stopped believing in me and my work. Thank you for reminding me often that I belong at the table, that I deserve good things, and that I am loved beyond measure. And thank you for reading an early draft of this book and saying, "This needs to be out there. You can't give up." It doesn't seem possible, but I love you more today than I did the day we married.

Thank you to my children, who understand my passion for writing stories and who are often the first readers of my work and give their blunt (unsolicited) opinions so unabashedly (and helpfully). I love you all more than you could possibly fathom.

Thank you to my parents, Kervin and Cherie Robinson, who are part of the happy ending in my story, and Jim and Shelly Patton, who helped forge my resilience and gave me my first magnificent summer. And thank you to Jarrod and Ashley, who made my childhood interesting and gave me plenty of humorous sibling experience to draw from.

Thank you to my friends Scott and Alana Ammons, Jared and Courtney Rawson, and Leigha Sutton, who listened to me cry and complain and wonder if my career was over while this book was out on submission. And to my therapist, for helping me through some of my lingering trauma so I could continue to write. And to the irreplaceable members of the Zoombie writing group, who meet every morning to work, collaborate, and discuss our professional and personal lives. Thank you, in particular, to Anne O'Brien Carelli, who always knows exactly the right words to say; Samantha M. Clark, who talked me through many dark days; and Sean Easley, whose superpower is kindness and encouragement.

Thank you to my agent, Rena Rossner, who took one look at this story and said, "This is your next book." Thank you for believing in me and Victoria, for guiding me and tolerating my exuberance, and most of all for understanding who I am and what I want to do with my life and career. Thank you for saying, "You can do this." Funny how such small words can feel so large.

Thank you to Kara Sargent, who fell in love with this story from the very beginning. Thank you for seeing what I wanted to do with Victoria's story and for sharing my vision and for taking such great care to make sure everything was as perfect as you knew I wanted it to be. Most of all, thank you for believing *The First Magnificent Summer* mattered enough to fight for its publication.

Thank you to all the team at Aladdin, including Valerie Garfield and Anna Jarzab, for getting the best of the best children's books into the hands of the readers who need them; Heather Palisi, for loving this story and taking such great care with the cover; Christina Pecorale, Emily Hutton, and the entire sales group for their incredible support; and the rest of the team behind this book: Olivia Ritchie, Sara Berko, Julie Doebler, Caitlin Sweeny, Nadia Almahdi, Ashley Mitchell, Alissa Nigro, Samantha McVeigh, Michelle Leo, and everyone else at S&S who believed in this book and worked so hard to help put it out in the world.

And thanks to Svetla Radioeva, for capturing the truest and most beautiful image of Victoria and her magnificent summer. Your work is astounding, and every time I look at this book, I smile. Thank you for seeing Victoria as I saw her.

Thank you to the many teachers and librarians and parents who put my books into the hands of young readers.

Last, but not least, thank *you*, my dear reader. I hope you always know how deeply loved you are.

There are not enough thank-yous in the world to properly express my gratitude. Have I forgotten someone? Probably. We don't do anything alone. So many have brought me to where I am today. So a broad thank-you to the many other giants in my life. I love and appreciate you all.